THE SINNERS

THE SINNERS

YUSUF IDRIS

TRANSLATED FROM THE ARABIC
BY KRISTIN PETERSON-ISHAQ

LYNNE
RIENNER
PUBLISHERS

BOULDER
LONDON

Contents

Published in the United States of America in 2009 by
Lynne Rienner Publishers, Inc.
1800 30th Street, Boulder, Colorado 80301
www.rienner.com

and in the United Kingdom by
Lynne Rienner Publishers, Inc.
3 Henrietta Street, Covent Garden, London WC2E 8LU

Cover art and drawings © Max Winkler.
First published in Arabic in 1959 as *al-Haram,* Cairo: al-Kitab al-Fiddi.
First published in English in 1984 by Three Continents Press, Inc.

ISBN 978-0-89410-394-0 (pbk. : alk. paper)

Printed and bound in the United States of America

The paper used in this publication meets the requirements
of the American National Standard for Permanence of
Paper for Printed Library Materials Z39.48-1992.

5 4 3 2

TRANSLATOR'S PREFACE

Yusuf Idris is one of the foremost figures in contemporary Arabic literature. He is best known as a short-story writer; indeed, he is probably the most prominent short-story writer in modern Egyptian literature.[1] He is, in addition, a playwright and the author of several novels. Of his novels, the best known is *The Sinners,* which is regarded as the greatest of all his longer stories.[2]

First published in 1959, the novel *The Sinners* (Arabic title, *al-Haram*) is distinguished by a special blend of local color and universal theme and is peopled by a rich variety of distinctive Egyptian characters. It represents the first attempt by an Egyptian writer to treat the plight of his country's seasonal workers.[3]

As a writer, Yusuf Idris is, first and foremost, a storyteller, and he presents the reader with no less than three stories within the framework of this short novel. Set on a large cotton estate in the Egyptian Delta region sometime before the 1952 Revolution, the work is dominated by the tragic tale of Aziza, a poverty-stricken migrant woman. She comes to work on the estate during the cotton season with her fellow migrant workers and there secretly gives birth to an illegitimate child. The novel opens with an estate guard's discovery of the newborn baby. The child is found dead, and from certain marks on the corpse, foul play is suspected. Much of the novel's early action concerns the efforts of the estate's year-around residents to discover the identity of the baby's mother, for they are sure that the mother and killer are one and the same. Leading the search and increasingly obsessed by it is the estate's chief administrative officer, Fikri Afendi. His compulsion to find the guilty woman is fueled by his conviction that the baby was murdered because it was born out of wedlock, making the woman doubly a sinner.

The estate's residents—the peasants and the employees who work in the administration—are convinced that the guilty party is one of the migrant workers who come to the estate during the cotton season each year. The estate residents greet the migrants' arrival every spring with a mixture of disdain and disgust, regarding them as a plague of noxious-smelling, miserable, half-human creatures whose presence must be borne because of the all-important cotton crop. The second story within the novel, then, focuses upon the estate's permanent residents. Interwoven with this and the story of Aziza is a third tale, that of the migrants. Through the three stories, Idris aims to achieve a twofold thematic purpose. First, he critically examines the conventional moral code, focusing the reader's attention upon Aziza's sin and the transformation which occurs in the estate residents' attitudes toward it. Second, he seeks to expose the injustice inherent in arbitrary class distinctions by detailing the migrant workers' grim circumstances.

The principal theme of the novel centers upon the concept of sin (al-haram). In Islamic law that which is divinely forbidden is haram.* In embodying this concept in the story in Aziza's illegitimate child, Idris tests the conventional moral code by confronting the estate's residents who profess to uphold it with a situation for which their rules do not provide. Fikri Afendi, for example, is driven to search for the mother of the illegitimate child not only because he wants to absolve the estate of moral and legal responsibility, but also because he harbors a secret desire to confront the sinner—and her sin—for himself. Sin as an abstract concept is one thing; sin that occurs practically on one's own doorstep has to be seen to be believed.

Unfortunately from the point of view of the estate's inhabitants, they are unable to locate the mother of the child among the migrant workers. Frustrated by their inability to pin the blame on the outsiders, they begin to eye one another with suspicion. As the search for the child's mother intensifies, the peasants discover how little they really know one another. Here the author explores the inner workings of the peasants' society, and his analysis of relationships within a small, isolated community is particularly well detailed. A case in point is his portrayal of Mesiha Afendi, the estate's chief clerk. Never before has Mesiha Afendi doubted his ability to enforce his strict moral code upon his family, but now he finds himself ready to convict his only daughter Linda—the estate's unrivaled beauty and the apple of his eye—on the basis of a stomach-ache.

The thickening atmosphere of suspicion and mistrust acts as a catalyst in the release of some long-suppressed emotions. Idris

---

*Similarly, the Arabic phrase "ibn haram" ("illegitimate child") has the literal meaning, "offspring of sin."

gives ironic life to this in his portrayal of Fikri Afendi's wife, Umm Safwat. A highly conventional woman of strict peasant upbringing, Umm Safwat finds herself on the verge of sinning, having become unsettled by the widespread preoccupation with the forbidden. In allowing herself to contemplate the possibility, she very nearly succumbs to temptation. The discovery of the illegitimate child and the subsequent frantic search for its mother also lead to a reaction among the estate's younger generation represented by Fikri Afendi's son, Safwat, his friend Ahmad Sultan, and the chief clerk's beloved daughter, Linda. Through his portrayal of estate society, Idris shows the peasants to be quite different from the smugly virtuous masks they wore when passing judgment on the unknown mother. It is this dimension that adds depth to the author's critical examination of the conventional moral code as he exposes the layers of hypocrisy within society, that hypocrisy which permits sin in all of its variations as long as the outward manifestations are suppressed.

Fikri Afendi's persistence is rewarded when he at last finds the criminal sinner he seeks. To add to his triumph (although he cannot quite bring himself to rejoice as he ought), she is a migrant woman; her name is Aziza. The estate residents are greatly relieved by what is nothing less than an acquittal of themselves and a vindication of what they had thought and said all along, and their contempt for the migrant workers increases. Curious to learn more about the unnatural creature who bore a child only to murder it, they make their way to the migrants' camp where the woman Aziza lies ill with fever.

Their malicious satisfaction at her misfortune turns to sympathy, however, when they learn the details of her story. Shaken out of their complacency by her suffering, they find that the rigid moral precepts they held have dissolved in the face of reality. Idris adds a final note of irony when he describes how a branch of willow intimately associated with Aziza and her illegitimate child takes root and grows into a tree that becomes known for its powers of healing, thus further blurring the line between sinner and saint.

The second theme addressed in *The Sinners* is closely linked to the first, for, just as Idris attempts to point out the inhumanity inherent in arbitrary moral judgments through Aziza's story, so, too, does he endeavor to reveal the inhumanity of arbitrary class distinctions through his portrayal of the migrant workers.

The migrant workers are landless poor who are driven to seek seasonal work far from their homes to earn a meager livelihood. They are called *Gharabwa* after their home province of Gharbiya and the peasants call them other names and make fun of their outlandish dialect. Where they are from is not important since there are many poor people from many poor villages and provinces in Egypt who endure brutal, backbreaking work for a pittance. Once the Gharabwa arrive on the estate, they live in virtual isolation in a camp behind the stables. There they are barely tolerated by the estate's permanent residents who do their best to ignore them. When Aziza is identified as the mother of the dead foundling, however, the migrants' existence is brought forcibly to everyone's attention and the estate inhabitants' aversion to them increases. They deeply resent the migrants who, having concealed Aziza's secret, allowed suspicion to make its way to the estate and indirectly caused the exposure of a number of secrets. Moreover, they now feel morally justified in their contempt for the migrant workers since it was a migrant woman who had sinned.

When the two groups meet around Aziza's sickbed, the estate residents begin to see the migrant workers in a different light. They are led in this by their children who, having yet to learn the prejudices of their elders, treat the migrant children as their equals. The new relationship starts with the exchange of a few words and develops as the people of the estate come to understand and accept the many bonds that link them to the Gharabwa. The change in attitude is most clearly demonstrated by the estate residents' behavior after Aziza's death: grief-stricken, the people of the estate come to the migrants' camp where they offer the migrants their condolences as to equals. Here the figure of Aziza can be seen to link the two themes. For, just as her suffering has caused the estate inhabitants to rethink their definition of sin, so, too, does her death assume greater significance through the change it has wrought in the relations of the estate residents and the Gharabwa.[4] Human nature may be subject to hypocrisy and prejudice, but it is nonetheless capable of change.

Fatma Moussa-Mahmoud has observed that "it is analytical interest in character that has given Idris his special place in Arabic letters."[5] His powers of characterization are well displayed in *The Sinners,* which is filled with a variety of characters realistically and vividly drawn with "astonishing insight into individual peasant characters."[6] The careful attention to detail which makes this emphasis on individuality possible is one of the most striking features of Idris' writing. Even minor figures display distinctive traits; major characters possess a complex mix of strengths and weaknesses which are portrayed in convincing detail.

Aziza, the central figure in the novel, is a sinner drawn with an aura of sainthood. Her character possesses near epic dimensions, complementing her tragic history. Aziza shows tremendous strength of character and an almost superhuman ability to endure pain and discomfort. Her dogged determination to support her family after her husband falls sick and her efforts to conceal her pregnancy at whatever physical cost to herself testify to these traits. Even when she becomes deathly ill, her only concern is that her family not go hungry.

Yet despite her strength and determination, Aziza yields to a moment of weakness, a moment for which she cannot forgive herself. When she is sexually assaulted in the incident which leaves her pregnant, she resists her attacker, but as she later admits to herself, not strongly enough, for there was a moment when she could have cried out or escaped and did not. Idris hints that it was the long period of sexual deprivation following her husband's illness that was chiefly responsible for her failure to take decisive action in the critical moment. In his writing Idris has more than once associated the ideas of sexual and psychological deprivation, and he appears to view them both as the result of social dispossession.[7] Aziza's sin can thus be seen, at least on one level, as an indirect product of the harsh social and economic conditions in which she exists.

Another complex character found in The Sinners is the estate commissioner, Fikri Afendi. The commissioner is a contradictory figure, at once shrewd and naive, exploitative and generous. He enjoys his position of power as estate manager and is not averse to ill-using his subordinates upon occasion. Yet, moved by Aziza's story, he endangers that same position by keeping her on the payroll and secretly arranges for the only medical treatment possible under the circumstances. An indulgent father and a despotic husband, Fikri Afendi reveals a many-sided character that is real and believable.

The chief clerk, Mesiha Afendi, is also portrayed as having more than one dimension. Cautious and reserved with the peasants and other employees, Mesiha has a deep affection for his family, especially his daughter Linda. His relationship with his wife Afifa is shown in marked contrast to that of Fikri Afendi and Umm Safwat.[8] Ambitious and fond of intrigue, the chief clerk is nonetheless moved by Aziza's plight and he abandons his plan to destroy Fikri Afendi's career.

Other characters, although less prominent, are drawn with sufficient detail to bring them vividly to life. Idris' style in *The Sinners* is simple and straightforward, and his use of language, while economical, is frequently striking. His realistic and objective treatment, combined with the careful attention to detail that is so much a feature of his work, succeeds brilliantly in evoking the atmosphere of a large, pre-revolutionary Egyptian estate and its many-layered society.

The author's use of humor, which ranges from gentle mockery to broad caricature, adds a distinctive flavor to the work. Idris also employs irony frequently and to effect. For example, he goes into a lengthy analysis of Mesiha Afendi's suspicions about his daughter's relationship with Safwat, which can be viewed as ironic preparation for the subplot involving Linda and Ahmad Sultan. Perhaps the most significant use of irony in *The Sinners* is the symbol of the willow tree. For, the women who come to the tree to be cured of childlessness are frequenting the site of sin itself. Thus, the willow tree symbolizes the transformation of sin into life which lies at the core of the author's vision while it serves as a link between the past and the present.

● ● ●

I initially chose to translate Yusuf Idris' novel *al-Haram* as part of my thesis work at the American University in Cairo. Translation is an eminently practical way for a student of literature to sharpen his skills and his understanding. Moreover, by seeking to reduce the linguistic barriers which separate peoples, it offers a means to contribute something tangible to one of literature's highest aims: increasing our understanding of our common humanity.

The need for translations of works of Arabic literature is particularly acute. The number of these works which have been translated into English is still relatively small, and this is a serious omission, particularly for the foreign student of the Arabic language. Few beginning students of Arabic have ready access to original works of literature in their field, for, unlike many other languages, Arabic usually requires a period of several years' intensive study before the student has acquired sufficient mastery to read and enjoy literary works on his own. Literary translations thus benefit the student by fulfilling a need for increased exposure to works of merit and by helping to demonstrate the vitality of the language and the culture it represents, thus increasing understanding and appreciation of both. The same may be said for general audiences who, though they may not have the student's specific motivation, do not lack the desire to learn more about another culture and way of life.

One of the cardinal principles of translation is not to translate anything one does not admire, and it was partially for that reason that I chose to translate a work by the contemporary Egyptian author Yusuf Idris. I have great respect for Dr. Idris as a short story writer, a novelist, and a playwright. Moreover, I feel that he has not received the attention he deserves from translators of modern Arabic literature. Such neglect is the more remarkable in view of the recognition Idris has achieved as a leading Egyptian writer who has, moreover, exerted considerable influence over the development of modern Arabic literature.

Although numerous technical difficulties are encountered in translating a literary work, perhaps the thorniest is how literal or how interpretive the translator should be. Does one try to remain completely faithful to the text, regardless of the cost to meaning in the translation? Should one aim at making a readable version and risk sacrificing some subtle, and some not so subtle, meanings in the original? There is, of course, no simple solution. I have tried to strike a balance between the two, attempting to make the translation as accurate as possible—including footnotes, for example, where I thought it advisable—while at the same time hoping it would be interesting to read.

Because this translation is meant for a general audience, I have omitted the diacritical marks which usually accompany the transliteration of Arabic proper nouns. I have tried to spell names in a way that will facilitate pronunciation for those who may be unfamiliar with Arabic, and in most cases, I have followed Egyptian colloquial usage. Standard spellings have been retained for those words which are familiar to English speakers, e.g., sheikh, tarboosh.

I am indebted to Dr. Hamdi Sakkut of the American University in Cairo for his patient encouragement and valuable help and advice while I was in Egypt. The librarians and staff members of the University's Center for Arabic Studies also deserve acknowledgment, especially Nabila al-Asyuti and Sumiya Saad. Dr. Yusuf Idris kindly allowed me to interview him when I was in Cairo, and he has continued to be most helpful. Dr. Donald Herdeck of

Three Continents Press also deserves acknowledgment for his assistance and encouragement. Finally, I thank my husband Mousa Ishaq for his untiring understanding and support.

Notes

[1] S. Somekh, "Language and Theme in the Short Stories of Yusuf Idris," *Journal of Arabic Literature* 6 (1975), 89.

[2] M. Abdel Salam, "The Longer Stories of Yusuf Idris" (unpublished M.A. thesis, American University in Cairo, 1973), 71.

[3] Ghali Shukri, *Azmat al-Jins fi l-Qissa al-Arabiya* (Beirut: Dar al-Adab, 1962), 254.

[4] Fatma Moussa-Mahmoud, *The Arabic Novel in Egypt (1914-1970)* (Cairo: Egyptian General Book Organization, 1973), 45.

[5] *Ibid.*, 43.

[6] *Ibid.*, 45.

[7] Shukri, 235.

[8] See Hilary Kilpatrick, *The Modern Egyptian Novel: A Study in Social Criticism* (London: Ithaca Press, 1974), 119.

YUSUF IDRIS

THE SINNERS

CHAPTER ONE

A moment of utter silence hung over that particular spot on the northern Delta where the estate stretches away so far that its end can hardly be seen. Night with its croaking and chirping was over, while the noisy clamor of full day was not yet near. The silence was as total as though the Resurrection* was about to take place, so awesome and sublime that even the tiniest creature seemed loath to break it. Only one thing disturbed the silence — a white ball diving and surfacing in the canal water, then plunging in again and each time producing a splashing sound that rose and echoed in the vast quiet.

This continued for some time until the white ball dove under and was gone longer than usual. Suddenly it emerged, cleaving the water with an even greater noise. At this time, it would have become clear to an observer that the ball was a forehead and it was not long before two eyes and a mouth appeared. Soon the face was complete and the head veered round, making its way to the bank. The closer it came, the more the water receded from a neck and then a body which was white in back and densely black in front. Near the bank arms appeared. Although they were thin in comparison with the heavy body, on the underside of the right one there was a tattoo of a girl holding a sword and some writing which, if looked at closely, would have spelled out a name. The name was Abd al-Muttalib Muhammad al-Bahraawi.

Abd al-Muttalib came out of the water. Although there were no living creatures in the entire area, he bent over and spread his joined hands to cover himself. Quickly he put on his clothes, a lot of worn-out garments which were finally held in place by a thick, yellow, venerable coat, a coat that had seen a full life. It had functioned as a tent with the Allies in the last World War, after which — like all veteran soldiers — it had come to a humble end.

---

*In Muslim theology, the Resurrection is a general resurrection of the world at the Last Judgment — Tr.

Finally Abd al-Muttalib performed the traditional morning prayer ritual. Then, hoisting the double-barreled shotgun onto his shoulder, he set off across the canal bridge, ambling along in his clumsy shoes made from cart tires.

On his way to the big farm, Abd al-Muttalib was suddenly stopped in his tracks by a strange white object which lay on one side of the bridge. He was excited since — like everyone else — as soon as Abd al-Muttalib caught sight of anything on the ground of a different color from the earth, he at once assumed that he had stumbled on a "find." His heart beat joyfully.

But, when he peered closer (although Abd al-Muttalib was a guard, his eyesight was none too good, especially in strong light), he saw what it was and stopped dead in his tracks. He was terrified and began to shout, "My God, my God, my God!"

For, the thing he had caught sight of was nothing other than a newborn baby!

Abd al-Muttalib's heart pounded loudly like a gunshot. Then he drew back, breathing heavily and still trembling. While it was true he was a guard, what he saw before him now was a very different matter from thieves and holdup men. His first impulse was to take to his heels, since he immediately assumed that what lay before him was some kind of evil spirit — a demoness's child no doubt.

However, Abd al-Muttalib did not run. Instead, a few seconds later he found himself laughing and harder than at any time in his life — since he was laughing at himself. Somehow he grasped the fact that the object in front of him was not an evil spirit nor anything of the kind. It was a baby — and a bastard, certainly. No sooner did that become clear to him than he burst into a loud guffaw. For some reason he concluded that the child was the result of his having spent the night before with his wife. ... After he had left her, to swim in the canal and make his morning ablutions, she had given birth to it and thrown it on the road.

It was an absurd thought, because of course his wife could not have become pregnant and given birth to a fully developed baby in one night. Still, he considered the possibility. When a human being is frightened, his mind may stop while he escapes with his body, or the opposite may take place: standing stock-still, he may escape with his mind, and the mind in its panic-stricken course is not restricted by any logic.

In any case, Abd al-Muttalib's laughter did not last long but was superseded by a sudden sense of responsibility. Although the spot where he had found the infant was not under his jurisdiction but under that of the granary guard, there are some people who no sooner find something wrong than they identify themselves with it. Such people feel responsible for it and start defending themselves to escape the responsibility. So Abd al-Muttalib was held captive in front of the foundling for that very reason, while plans whirled in his head of how to defend himself before other people, the estate commissioner and — God forbid — the prosecuting attorney and the courts.

While Abd al-Muttalib was thus engaged, the uppermost arc of the sun was beginning to turn yellow, then white, and spread rays along the horizon as though reconnoitering. When it was assured that everything was all right, the sun's enormous red bulk came out as though from behind the arc. As the sun rose, the world began to stir and call all its creatures to wakefulness and work. The white egret began to screech and flap its wings, and people started to appear, scattered individuals at first coming from the mosque after prayers or making their way to the canal to wash their faces and to bathe.

As the world awoke, Abd al-Muttalib began to regain his presence of mind, his brain started to clear. He failed to rid himself completely of responsibility, but a certain idea occurred to him.

Why shouldn't he throw the bundle into the canal? There wasn't anyone around to see him, and no one would be any the wiser. He vacilated a moment between ye-e-es and no-o-o and then approached the bundle with excessive caution. At the same instant he was startled by a voice, rough as an acacia branch, saying, "Good morning, Abdu."

Abd al-Muttalib stared round vaguely, because he was fair and blear-eyed with small, narrow eyes that only saw well at night. He stared and uttered the phrase for which he was famous, "Confound you and everyone else!"

His words came out enveloped in little clouds of morning vapor. The newcomer was Atiya. No one knew when or from where he had first come to the estate. For as long as he had lived there, he had had no known occupation — no, not even a place to live, since he slept wherever chance offered. You always saw him clutching the end of the long, shirtlike garment which hung below his knees but revealed his hairless shanks. When he talked to a person, he opened one eye and shut the other, staring at him or her from the narrow face that no one trusted.

Puffs of vapor continued to emerge from Atiya's mouth and were answered in kind from Abd al-Muttalib's, while their hands gestured now at the bundle and then at the canal, the people, the farm and the skies above. Finally they were joined by a third man, Usta Muhammad. Usta Muhammad was undisputedly the "man of events" on the estate, since not a single important incident took place there without his being the first on the scene. No one knew how the news reached him, but you could be sure to find him on the spot.

Usta Muhammad was an old man of over seventy, with a white, sprouting beard, white hair and a left eye whose closed lid never lifted. He had been a machine foreman on the estate and, when he became too old to work, was fired. In spite of this, he was occasionally called in to start the engine that drove the threshing machine or to stay up late by the water pump. He was still called usta,* in any case, and he was still the "man of events" whose opinion about whatever incidents occurred was regarded as the right one. This time he no sooner learned what had happened and had looked at the baby with his good right eye, than he said, "That isn't dead, Abdu ... that's strangled."

Abd al-Muttalib's mind refused to accept this at first. It did not take Usta Muhammad long to convince him, however, by pointing out the body's blueness and a certain reddening around the nose and mouth, and then to ask him to clear himself of all responsibility by notifying the agricultural inspector, since he was the only person able to act in such matters.

Abd al-Muttalib was apparently convinced. Chewing on his lip, he presently said, "Yes, the best way is for us to notify the commissioner."

As he spoke no more clouds of vapor were emitted. The sun had grown stronger, bodies were warming up, and the dew had begun to evaporate.

---

*Usta is a colloquial Egyptian word which means "master (of a trade); foreman, overseer." It is also used as a form of address to those in such callings as cabdriver, wagoner, etc. — Tr.

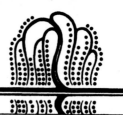

CHAPTER TWO

No one knew just how the news filtered through to the farm. The three men became six and in no time were surrounded by a crowd of laborers on their way to the fields, with mattocks on their shoulders and their lunches in handkerchiefs. Soon they were joined by threshing machine workers, farmers and some children who had been woken by their fathers and forced down to the canal to wash their faces.

Even the women left whatever they were doing, putting down the dough, bread or clay that was in their hands, and hurried breathlessly to the canal, bedaubing the men whom they pushed apart, to see what was to be seen.

Every new arrival wanted to see the bastard child that had just been found dead. He would push and shove until he got through and could stare at it, drinking in the details of the white skin which had turned first blue, then almost black, and the small head smeared with blood and shreds of the placenta. The sight would soon make him turn and go away in a depressed state of nausea and dread, which showed on his face and his entire bearing.

The agricultural commissioner arrived finally and eager hands pushed everyone else aside to make way for him. The commissioner, Fikri Afendi, had no less desire to witness this incident (which was a novel one for both him and the farm) than anyone else. At the same time he was careful not to let his excitement diminish his dignity. As soon as he drew near the crowd, he raised his hand and carefully tilted his tarboosh to the proper angle. Then his dark features assumed a solemn expression and he stretched his neck arrogantly in the way he liked to look in the eyes of the peasants. Then suddenly his eyes fell on the object of the scene and he was unable to conceal the dread and nausea that overwhelmed him, too. These feelings showed plainly in his lips' nervous quivering and the haste with which he turned at once to leave.

The commissioner was followed by the overseer, the irrigation guard, Tantaawi, Usta Muhammad and a few of the day laborers and workers. They moved along silently and gloomily while the commissioner spat alternately into his white, screwed-up handkerchief and the wet straw on the road.

CHAPTER THREE

Commissioner Fikri Afendi's duty could have ended right there. He might be responsible for every event that took place on the estate, but to find a dead — or murdered — baby and try to discover its killer was something that did not enter into his jurisdiction at all.

Actually that was what he was thinking as he walked unhurriedly along the road to the estate's administration buildings followed by the small group of men. Still, a certain curiosity did begin to rise in him. Whose baby could this be, he wondered.

The estate was composed of several farms, but not one of them had more than thirty houses. The foundling had been discovered beside the big farm's canal which ran near the owners' mansion and the administration buildings. There were found the stables, the threshing floor, the storehouses, and the garages for the tractors. The foundling, then, must definitely be the child of a woman from the big farm, and Fikri Afendi knew almost every one of its young girls and its women individually. Which one of them had done this thing? How had she done it?

Fikri Afendi had frequently heard about illegitimate children in stories and gossip. Scandals like the present one reached him occasionally but only as news about people he did not know. He had no idea what they would look like or what sort of people they were. Deep inside himself, even if he had read the news in the *Muqattam* newspaper itself (every word of which he believed wholeheartedly), he would have found himself scarcely able to believe it — scarcely able to believe that forbidden, shocking, and serious events such as rape or illegitimate pregnancy could actually occur. Yet, today with his own eyes, he had seen a complete and dead *corpus delicti* almost stick out its finger and poke it in the eye of each and every incredulous person.

Strange sensations overcame him as he stood staring at the little body. It was like seeing the very forbidden thing which he refused to believe existed, or refused to believe the possibility of people being audacious enough to do. Right in front of his eyes he had seen it as it lay in the flesh on the canal bank. A number of different feelings struggled within him. The forbidden, then, does exist in people, and sometimes they are unable to hide it. Sometimes it even defeats them, conquers their wish for concealment, and shows itself embodied in a baby's shrouded corpse or a swollen belly. The forbidden thing you've heard about, Fikri Afendi, and never believed in, does exist, and here you are with a good chance of seeing the woman who did it, just as you saw it itself.

It was that very thought that kept occurring to him on his way back to the administration building. What could she be like, the woman who committed this forbidden act — or, more precisely, the whore? Not once had he heard that word mentioned without feeling a shiver run through his body. Although Fikri Afendi, like most people, had had relationships with women before he got married and even afterwards, he found it hard to believe that there were women in the world who sinned like those who did so with him — as though the women who sinned with him were not whores — only those who sinned with others.

I wonder what this woman is like and if she's beautiful. Does she look like a dancing girl? Is she like other women, or does she in fact have special tricks and insinuating gestures to lure some wolf of a man off alone with her and commit with her — God forgive me for thinking it! — the forbidden?

Fikri Afendi stopped halfway between the canal and the administration building and turned. The group of men who followed him did likewise. He began to study the big farm which lay before him with its dark houses, and the smoke that had started to rise from the many chinks and crannies in the roofs. At the verge of the farm stood the house of Mesiha Afendi, the chief clerk. Next to it was that of the clerk, Ahmad Sultan, the fair young man who wore his dark tarboosh at a rakish tilt and a clean, black coat. An attractive young fellow, he was often caught winking at one of the well-developed older girls who sometimes came to work on the estate. His wink always electrified a girl and made her breasts dance.

But Fikri Afendi was not looking for someone who might be suspected of being the father. He was searching for the mother. For, although he was prepared to believe in the existence of the forbidden in men, he somehow found it hard to believe in women. A man's role in the forbidden was fleeting, a woman's was basic. He was looking for the mother. He left no one out of his mental investigation — not even the chief clerk's wife, Umm Linda. But she had visited his own wife last week and had not looked at all pregnant.

8

His eyes roved from house to house: those which belonged to the big farmers who had more than three pairs of livestock each and those of the day laborers who owned nothing but their mattocks. All the women on the farm passed one by one in review before his eyes: her he knew well and her he hardly knew, her who laughed and smiled and her who wore a red kerchief or a brightly colored *gallabiya**, the young girl and the old maid, the single woman, the divorcee, and the woman of doubtful reputation, her who once responded to his teasing and her who was embarrassed and did not.

Fikri Afendi's gaze did not come to rest on a single house or a particular woman. For, there was no one "in hiding" on the farm. All of the women went out even without wearing a *malas**** over their colored dresses. Moreover, they were all well known. No one had noticed that an unmarried woman was pregnant or showed any signs of it. It was impossible for any of them to be that baby's mother — impossible.

Gallabiya is the Egyptian colloquial word for an ankle-length, loose-fitting garment. Wide-sleeved and collarless, the *gallabiya* is worn by the more traditional members of Egyptian society — Tr.

**The word *malas* refers to a thin outer garment worn by traditional Egyptian women. Made of silk and dyed black, it is generally worn by the relatively prosperous — Tr.

The commissioner awoke from his long contemplation of the farm and its inhabitants. Next he turned his eyes to the faces of the few men gathered around him, paused and stared at each one for a moment. At every pause a face would grow pale, since the men themselves almost doubted their own innocence. Each was almost unnerved by thinking the commissioner might keep on staring at him and would suddenly point at him and say, "You."

However, the commissioner only stared for the purpose of speculative thought and to verify the soundness of the opinion he had formed.

Suddenly Fikri Afendi gestured with the cane he had with him. Pointing at the open area behind the stables, he cried, "It must be one of them."

The men's eyes and hearts turned in the direction he indicated and the answer sprang from most of them like a cry of acquittal "Them. It's nobody but them. Why, it's obvious. They're Gharabwa* and sons of bitches."

They said this in unison and readied themselves to a man for any order the commissioner might give.

However, the commissioner gave no order, having gone back to staring at his faded shoes while his cane played idly once again with his shoelaces and the straw.

Then he said, "It's possible it could be Nabawiya."

Saalih, the overseer, immediately changed the direction of his mind and spoke up. "Why not? ... She sells eggs, doesn't she? And she's a big flirt."

Then Usta Muhammad observed, "She's been single a long time. ... Who knows, it's possible — God forgive me for saying it."

And Abd al-Muttalib, the guard, said, "I'm certain it's her."

The commissioner did not give them much time, however. He soon turned, and his eyes roved back and forth until they came to rest on the area behind the stables. Then he said, "Not at all. It has to be them and nobody else."

The men standing around him muttered and cursed the Gharabwa in agreement.

---

*"Gharabwa" is the Egyptian colloquial word for the inhabitants of the Egyptian province of al-Gharbiya. In the context of this novel, "Gharabwa" is synonymous with "migrant workers" — Tr.

CHAPTER FOUR

The Gharabwa. They were not residents of the estate, nor was it possible for anyone to imagine their ever living there. Weren't they the poorest people of their own region who, driven by poverty to work on far-off estates, left their homes and their villages for the sake of a daily wage of no more than a few piasters? Weren't they those wretched people who wore ragged clothing and had a strange smell? It was impossible for anyone to imagine people like that living on the estate. The estate inhabitants were all respected farmers. Everyone had a house, children, livestock and a clean new *gallabiya* to wear after work when he stayed up late in the coffeehouse or went to weddings and funerals. Moreover, no one on the estate was ever out of work since the farms were built to absorb all the peasants, like a big factory that had a section set aside to house its workers.

Consequently, everyone on the estate worked, and they all had some money. When a woman got married, she brought to her husband a bed, a wardrobe, a set of china and sometimes a sewing machine. Nor was the estate work hard enough to be unbearable. Irrigation was done with machines, plowing by tractor and huge machines took care of the threshing — machines· which by themselves took up half the threshing floor. True, the estate took most of what the land produced but still, the peasant had enough left over to feed and clothe and shelter him. But this also inevitably made him regard the Gharabwa as miserable human refuse obliged to leave their homes in order to find work, in order to eat and make some kind of life for themselves. No one even agreed on their name. The administration called them "migrant workers," while the peasants called them "Gharabwa." Then, there were those who were sarcastic and ridiculed their way of life and gave them a long,

derisive name by means of which, in order to make fun of their speech, they imitated the way the migrant workers pronounced their k's like j's. That was how much the estate peasants despised the migrant workers' k, their dialect, and their very presence on "their" estate.

The Gharabwa themselves did not take much notice of how the peasants regarded them or of their ridicule — as though they accepted being Gharabwa, migrant workers, or anything else that occurred to people to call them. As long as they had won a place for themselves among the seasonal workers which guaranteed steady, paying work for more than three months, let people say what they liked.

Cotton is planted at the end of winter. Almost at once, as soon as the Coptic month of Tuba is over, the seeds split and penetrate the brown earth, each one sprouting a root and a stem. Discussion centers on the migrant workers as soon as the cotton shoots have covered wide, black areas with their lushly beautiful layer of green. Now is the time for the cotton worm to start hatching. Fikri Afendi would write a letter to the administration in Cairo which would reply in kind. Then the authorization follows, and so does the money.

On a certain morning, Fikri Afendi would wake up early. He would take the first train, changing at Tanta, and then travel by bus (never forgetting to enter it in his expense account as a taxi) to a village in the province of Munufiya or Gharbiya. Which one does not matter since Fikri Afendi is acquainted with many villages and many contractors. He calls the villages "anthills," because they have so many people — more than are needed, more than the demand for work and the existing food supply. All of them are poor, too — so poor that Fikri Afendi shakes his head in sorrow when he sees them in their villages and observes the way they live.

Anyway, the news of his arrival spreads in a swift and mysterious way as soon as he sets foot in the village. Hundreds of people gather and form a procession. They troop along ahead, behind and on both sides of him, all the while gazing at him in fervent hope, as though he carried sacks of life soon to be handed out to them. Greeting him, they scramble to touch him and catch his eye — the smart man is the one who first shakes his hand, then kisses it. A thousand people lead him to the contractor's house even though he has no need of a guide. For years now he has come to this village, and no one can get lost on the way to the contractor's house in such a small place — no one, that is, like Fikri Afendi who has been endowed with intelligence, know-how, a tarboosh and in fact the devil's own cunning.

He finds the contractor standing at the threshold of his house, if the noise of Fikri Afendi's arrival has not reached him first and brought him to stand at the head of the street. Hearty and demonstrative greetings take place, nor is there any objection to a tear escaping the contractor's eye as he sighs over the good old days gone by. The man insists on calling Fikri Afendi "Honored Inspector," and Fikri Afendi, embarrased, says modestly, "Now, now, Hagg*." The necks of many ducks and pigeons are surrendered, and the commissioner eats, has dessert and then rests. Afterwards he sips his coffee and pleasurably exhales the smoke of the cigarette pressed on him by the contractor who swears — or he'll divorce his own wife — that he must smoke it.

Meanwhile, the uproar outside the house increases. The horde of ants stream out of their holes, now that a chance of work has appeared. They hug each other in front of the house and shout back and forth, "This is a lucky day, men. Things are going to be great!"

The guest and his host argue a little, even a great deal, about the wages, the commissioner saying that each laborer will get seven piasters and that, plus a piaster commission for the contractor, makes eight. The contractor insists on ten. "That'll be too much for the landowners to swallow," the commissioner says. It ends up at maybe nine. The commissioner takes out his wallet, feeling pleasure and then slight dismay as the large, green ten-pound notes with the picture of the minaret touch his hand only long enough to be counted and then vanish into the contractor's linen pouch, a pouch that has a crescent and three stars painted on it, under which is printed — no one knows why — "the Egyptian Government." Hardly is the transaction complete than self-appointed town criers run off through the village: "It's six piasters a man, everybody, and you get paid every fifteen days. Everybody here tell those that are gone." There is no need for a public announcement since "everybody" is there, crowded together in front of the contractor's house, on neighboring rooftops, and in front of adjacent doors.

Next morning five big trucks draw up specially licensed to transport laborers (just like the special licenses for transporting bags of rice or livestock). Each one carries more than a hundred men, women and children along with their bundles and the baskets they have filled to overflowing with bread and tall clay jars of whey and

---

*"Hagg" is the honorific title given to a Muslim who has made the pilgrimage to Mecca, the holiest city of Islam — Tr.

cheese. They are crowded together in a solid mass, so tightly packed you can hardly tell a man from a woman or a boy from an earthenware jar.

As the trucks roll out, from the throats of those so crushed and crowded together bursts song and laughter, a joyous uproar that rises to the sky. ... Meanwhile, the eyes of the sick and disabled, of all those who cannot carry a mattock or bend a back, the eyes of those who must stay behind because their number exceeds the demand, these eyes watch the triumphant procession which, little by little, is nearing the world of work where there will be a salary, a bite to eat, and deep, long drags of smoke on a narghile.* They watch it in tearful helplessness and sorrow; perhaps one man consoles his neighbor with the mild word "patience."

Thick clouds of dust that fill the horizon announce the arrival of the trucks at the estate. But their coming attracts little attention. All that happens is that someone may stand and watch the incoming trucks and say (with a sarcastic laugh to anyone around) that long, j-filled nickname which they use to ridicule the Gharabwa.

Once there behind the stable, the Gharabwa stack their baskets in neat rows. Then off they go to the threshing floor and the nearby land to collect rice straw and stones to make beds and fires.

---

*A narghile is a tobacco pipe by which the smoke is drawn through water by means of a long tube — Tr.

Before sunrise the next day the smell of whey fills the air, its containers having been opened. Every once in a while the sound of an onion being split is heard, or a low murmuring, or the cries of a girl who has failed to find her supplies. The persistent tapping of the boss's cane on someone's basket to hasten the end of the meal and the beginning of the march is also heard. Before long the tapping moves from straw baskets to the backs of heads and to bodies, but it is never more than a light rat-a-tat. Finally he yells, and the migrant workers get up and move forward in one huge, dark-skinned body, trailed by scattered individuals. The procession is the first to set foot on the dew-drenched path. By the time the sun rises each one is in charge of a row. Inevitably, everyone's back is bent, his eyes riveted on the eggs of the cotton worm.

Every evening before sunset, Junaidi Abu Khalaf's store is packed, since it is the only store on the big farm. It is jammed with earthenware dishes held in dry, outstretched hands, with voices roughened by the cotton branches, voices which, in their awkward Gharabwa dialect, ask persistently for "three *mallims'* worth of oil ... a *mallim's* worth of salt ... a quarter-piaster's worth of honey ... a half-piaster's worth of cigarette papers. ..." Junaidi curses both the Gharabwa and the day they came, but he sells. He damns their fathers and continues to sell, while their rust-worn *mallims* and *niklas* (they are all *mallims* and *niklas*; the biggest coin they have is a ten-*mallim* piece*) pile up in his greasy drawer.

Exactly at sunset before dark, a mingled aroma rises from behind the stables, of frying oil, grilled fish, matured white cheese, lentils, onions and carbolic soap. These individual smells blend together in a strange and penetrating whole, to create a distinctive odor which, because of its strong connotation and pungent quality, the peasants call "the migrant workers' smell." The smells rise, jars are opened and everything that can possibly be plucked from the field (radishes, chicory and varieties of wild plants) is laid out. Stomachs are stuffed with all this in the same way as bags are packed full of rice. Silence descends on the camp. All that can be heard in this silence is the sounds of jaws moving as they chew on mouthfuls of bread and of a few spoons scraping the brass containers to pick off the last grains of rice sticking to the bottom.

---

*The Egyptian pound is officially valued at approximately $1.45 (U.S.). A piaster (*qirsh*) equals 1/100 of an Egyptian pound. The *nikla* is equal to two *mallims*, and a single *mallim* is the smallest monetary unit in Egypt, equalling 1/1000 of a pound — Tr.

The wind carries the noise and the smell to the big farm and its inhabitants crack jokes, laugh uproariously and are more than ever convinced that these are really and truly the dregs of humanity ... those people ... those they call the migrants.

CHAPTER FIVE

Fikri Afendi drew a circle in the dust with his cane. Putting a dot in the center, he made lines radiating out from it to the circle's circumference. Then he erased it. He even ground his heel into it until all that was left was the central dot with a few broken lines e-merging. ... He had no clear plan in mind, for even supposing that he had narrowed down the choice of a culprit to one of the Gharabwa, what could he possibly do to find her? He racked his brains, the cane tapping against his yellow trouser leg and his weary eyes lost in thought. If it was one of the Gharabwa women who did it, then she must be resting up in the migrants' camp. She had to be. It was inconceivable that a woman could give birth to a child, kill it or have it die on her, and then go to work in the cotton field the next morning. That fact put him in a position to find out; all he had to do was make sure.

Fikri Afendi frowned, a sure sign of his having come to a decision, and started out for the migrants' camp, accompanied by the small group of men. The camp was deserted, since the laborers had left for the field before sunrise as usual, and there was nothing there but baskets, dead campfires, charred fragments of wood, and the smells of sunset. Fikri Afendi and the men with him took this in at a glance, but the commissioner decided to look the camp over, just in case. Head bent and hands holding the cane behind his back, he began to prowl about. From time to time, he sniffed the air, and struck the baskets and supply sacks, to be on the safe side. He kept this up, the group of men following him, until they came upon the woman whom the farm children called "Old Mother Migrant." The woman was so old that no one knew her exact age. But despite her advanced years, she worked just as the laborers did, and collected a half-day's pay. Her job, however, was easier, since she guarded the migrant workers' bundles and other necessities, and watched over the children until their mothers returned to camp at the end of the day. Fikri Afendi stopped in front of the old woman and fought back a smile to see her surrounded by dozens of children, some in her lap, and the rest scattered among the bundles. A few of the children were screaming; the others, calm, quiet and sensible, were playing with the woman's dress and feet. He fought back a smile, because the old woman looked so anxious and bewildered. She was obviously at a loss to know what to do or say to the children, or how to feel affection for them, since so much time had intervened between her and the qualities of motherhood and child-care.

Fikri Afendi tried vainly to win a response from the old woman to his questions. In a stupor from old age and feebleness, she achieved a state of awareness only when a stranger approached the camp — at which time she would scream at him to go away — or when the mothers returned before sunset, creating an uproar that would end as every mother slipped away with her child. Other times the commotion did not end, and the old woman would go off, stumbling, to search with a mother whose child had gotten lost among the bundles. ...

Fikri Afendi did not even need to question the old woman, for there was no one in the camp. That meant one of two things: either the criminal had forced herself to go to work with the laborers so she wouldn't be discovered, or she wasn't one of the Gharabwa and might be from the farm.

Fikri Afendi stopped short at the latter possibility, and began to stare once again at the open area, scrutinizing it with one eye open and the other half-shut, and shaken, uneasy thoughts. He was as sure the culprit was a migrant woman as he was of the Day of Resurrection and the blame-casting soul.* But there was a slight chance she could be from the farm, especially since the migrants' camp was clean. It was the merest possibility, a one-in-a-thousand chance, but there it was, and he must check it out. Only a short while ago he had studied the farm, and decided its women were all innocent. Still, it was possible — very possible — he had overlooked or forgotten someone who might be the criminal.

Deep in thought, the commissioner did not notice the approach of Saalih, the agricultural overseer. He didn't become aware of him until Saalih's woolen skullcap over which he wore a turban was right under his noise, and Saalih whispered with a smile and a sly, leering

---

*This phrase is taken from the Quran, Chapter LXXV (Chapter of the Resurrection), v. 1 and 2:

1. I swear not by the resurrection day;
2. I swear not by the blame-casting soul;

(From The Quran, tr. by Richard Bell, Vol. II. Edinburgh: T. and T. Clark, 1939, p. 620) — Tr.

look, "Why couldn't it be Nabawiya?"

Although he spoke in a whisper, everyone heard him. The men's voices rose, protesting what he had said and insisting it was the Gharabwa they wanted, all but swearing to it by the Quran. They denounced the accuser and the charge, and went on to tell, with a word from here and another from there, the story of Nabawiya. She was the wife of one of the wagoners on the estate who died and left her with his horse and wagon, and a girl and a boy. Selling the horse and wagon, she went into the tomato business with the proceeds. Later she went broke and worked as a contractor of laborers, and baked bread for others on the farm. After that she was a maid in the former commissioner's house, and now she sold eggs. She raised the girl and the boy, and even sent the boy to be educated in the local Quran school. She did not neglect either of her children, nor was she overly permissive with them. What she permitted herself, however, was the subject of much debate and conjecture. The men's voices rose in protest; meanwhile they watched the commissioner to see the discussion's effect on him. When his face remained unconvinced, they began to back down, or so it appeared. One man said, "God only knows what's hidden, men." Another replied, "The Devil's clever."

However, Nabawiya herself, easily distinguishable from the other farm women by her ample posterior and thick, silver ankle bracelets worn so tightly they nearly stopped the circulation in her plump legs, soon silenced all tongues when she was spotted by the commissioner and the men standing around him. A basket on her arm, she was seen knocking on doors and selling eggs, the picture of perfect health. All eyes turned to Saalih in malicious pleasure, their gaze so penetrating it all but pierced his woolen skullcap, white turban and heavy, black *gallabiya* that was never changed. Saalih busied himself by reaching into his pocket and taking out a tin of tobacco. Then he retired to a distant spot — by way of good manners — and proceeded to roll a cigarette. ...

When the commissioner saw Nabawiya, his expression grew dark. Annoyed, he made haste to leave the spot, shouting, "Abd al-Muttalib, get my donkey!"

The only remaining hope was to find the woman among the migrants who were working in the field.

The donkey arrived a short while later. It was a sleek, plump animal, so well-fed the hamstring did not show, and its white coat was unblemished by so much as a single black hair. When it moved, the bridle jingled, and its step had the noble grace of a thoroughbred.

19

The commissioner faced Abd al-Muttalib's shoulder, and with a mighty heave of his body, which nearly made the guard fall to his knees, he mounted the elegant, covered saddle.

Scarcely did the donkey feel its rider sitting straight in the saddle than it brayed long and proudly. Then it took off, and all the overseers, a few of the day laborers, Abd al-Muttalib, and old Usta Muhammad began to run in pursuit.

CHAPTER SIX

By that time the sun had left the tops of the tall eucalyptus trees planted like a solemn fence around the estate, and begun to quicken its pace toward the middle of the sky. The track the manager followed was bare and lifeless. Unshaded by any tree and unrelieved by even a blade of grass, it was nothing more than a thick line of dirt, with hundred of *feddans** to the right of it and hundreds more to the left. The field was quiet, infinitely quiet, its silence the kind that buzzes stubbornly and persistently, always reminding you of its presence. The only sound that broke the silence was the pounding of the donkey's hooves as they hit the ground, one after the other, and, nearly sinking in the soft dirt, stirred up clouds of dust.

The dust, as persistent and as biting as flies, assailed the faces of the men who panted along behind the commissioner and his donkey. A pitiless sun began to grill their heads and backs, but not even draping themselves with the ends of their long robes helped them ward off its fiery blaze. Even Fikri Afendi stuck a handkerchief under his tarboosh in an effort to shade his face. He kicked the donkey a couple of times, and then gave it a sharp poke with the pointed end of his cane to which, with that very purpose in mind, he had fastened a small nail. He jabbed the animal right in the withers; the donkey, however, did not need to be kicked or prodded, since it was racing along as fast as it could.

The small procession continued to sweep along the path, while it — with its commissioner, the men who followed him, and even the clouds of dust it raised — was nothing more than a small, moving dot in that vast, sunlit expanse which went on forever. Onward toiled the procession in silence. The donkey panted, and the men puffed as their sweat streamed down. Even Fikri Afendi, the only one riding, poured with sweat. The procession continued on for some time, and then it seemed that old Usta Muhammad suddenly realized that

---

*The *feddan* is a square measure of land (somewhat larger than an acre) which equals 4,200.833 m^2 — Tr.

none of this was any of his business. Washing his hands of the foundling, he stopped running, and sat down by the edge of the road to catch his breath. He sat on the short grass that grew along the canal bank, as though he were an old bush that had suddenly sprung up in its midst. And it was not long before he did exactly as the clumps of grass on which he sat. Just as they reached out with their roots to the running water, so, too, did he stretch out his legs and feet, and immerse them in the canal as if to water his very soul that had nearly succumbed to the blazing heat of the sun.

The rest of the caravan went on its way as though unaware that the old man had fallen behind, for everyone in it was busy with his own misery and sweat.

Not once had Fikri Afendi mounted his donkey and ridden off to the field — something he did every day — without pleasure. The donkey did not walk, it danced, and every movement it made was full of noble pride and grace. But this time he was too preoccupied by the morning's crisis to enjoy the ride, or even to notice his sweat, the heat, and the men panting behind him. For the first time, he was forced to think about something totally different from his job as agricultural inspector, and that was all he thought of. He must consider something entirely removed from seeds, manure, and land that was either too dry or urgently needed to be fertilized. For, now it was the migrant workers he had to reflect on, and not as he usually thought about them, either. As a matter of fact, normally he thought about them only as laborers — farmhands who picked off worms, harvested cotton, and dredged drainage ditches. The gray-haired old man was a laborer, and so was the little boy. They were all the same: feet that were cracked from hunger and walking barefooted, calloused by the unyielding earth; thin, sunburned hands; and grim faces whose sorrow you couldn't tell from joy, just as you couldn't see the difference between a man and a woman. Even their clothing was the same: old people's, youngsters', the man's *gallabiya* that had turned color and was full of holes, and the woman's faded, black dress with its fraying threads. It often happened that a Gharabwa man would borrow his wife's long robe, she would wear his *gallabiya*, and no one would know the difference.

Fikri Afendi had gotten used to seeing them like this. True, he assumed the wrongdoer was one of them, told everyone that was so, and went himself to search behind the stable, but it was as if he did all that without thinking. In actual fact, he was unable to imagine that in that human herd there was a woman who was worthy of being called female.

He was certain the culprit was among them, but still he found it impossible to believe that these Gharabwa women could have babies, legitimately or otherwise. He could not believe it, as though the person who had borne the foundling was, incredibly, not a woman, but a man.

He was compelled, then, as the sun burned his head despite the handkerchief and tarboosh, to believe this and to start looking at the migrant workers from another angle. True, they were laborers and Gharabwa, but there were women among them who got pregnant and had babies. What was more, they did so illicitly. ...

The thought did not make Fikri Afendi's mind rest easier, by any means, because it was hard for him to change the way he looked at the migrant workers in a moment. It was also difficult to transform his mental image of a laborer into a woman who slept with men, got pregnant, and had children. Fikri Afendi, however, was the sort of person who did not usually let facts disturb him too much before believing them. So be it. Let the culprit be a migrant. He would just have to find her, see her with his own eyes, and decide how she could have done this thing. Fikri Afendi didn't even wait until he got to the laborers, for his thoughts began to wander and precede him, going back in time before today's incident as he imagined — and there was pleasure accompanying his thoughts — the story that had ended with that morning's scene. With his imagination, he spied on the story in no little embarrassment, prepared to stop at any moment. Then he began to lose himself in the tale of love that had doubtless developed between the girl and one of the handsome, bare-chested, strapping young migrants, how he had crept stealthily to her one night, and what was to be, was. ...

The donkey stumbled and nearly fell, but checked itself powerfully. At the same time, Fikri Afendi's roving imagination tripped over something which occurred to him just then, and he was overcome with indignant fury. This meant the sin was committed on estate land. He didn't own the estate, and he certainly wasn't its defender of virtue, but the mere thought was enough to put him in a rage, making him beat the donkey heavily with his cane to punish it for having stumbled. Yet, even as his indignation reached its height, he did not forget entirely that the baby they had found that day was fully developed and that the migrant workers had been on the estate for no more than two months. Here only did F̶i̶k̶r̶i̶ ̶A̶f̶e̶n̶d̶i̶ ̶s̶t̶o̶p̶ beating and goading the donkey, and experience ̶a̶ ̶b̶r̶e̶e̶z̶e̶ blowing gently upon him from the heart. The crim̶e̶ ̶d̶i̶d̶ ̶n̶o̶t̶ take place there. The girl was "poorly" when sh̶e̶ estate, and, when the evil reached completion in her belly, she delivered it in the dead of night without commotion or anyone having noticed. And then for no reason she strangled it.

What a whore!

Nor did she stop at that, but forced herself to go to work with the others in the early dawn so no one would guess her guilty secret.

What an amazon!

Fikri Afendi kicked the donkey hard as he passed a hand over his face to wipe off the sweat that had collected around his mouth and trickled from the end of his nose, saying in a muted roar, "God help us!"

CHAPTER SEVEN

The donkey brayed loudly. Its bray was unlike that of any other donkey. All the people on the estate knew the sound and could have picked it out from among thousands of donkeys, because they all broke into a cold sweat when they heard it.

And not for the first time, Fikri Afendi was thoroughly put out. In his opinion, that bray was his donkey's one fault. It was as though it had some kind of a pact with the contractors, laborers, and overseers. As soon as he went out on a tour of inspection, intending to catch everyone unawares, the donkey would surprise him with that bray — a sound so loud it would carry to the ends of the earth, awaken sleepers from their beds, and ensure that everything in the field would be in perfect order and total readiness to receive him.

The donkey brayed as the procession, having just left the wheatfield, began to enter the land that was planted with cotton. The field was so vast that it overwhelmed you to learn that one person owned it all, and you immediately wished you were that person. The look of the cultivated field was sure to make you think of heaven, and as you walked along the path, you saw the nearby canal and the cotton branches in full with their leaves and bolls. But as you moved farther away, the cotton plants merged and blended until the square in front of you suddenly seemed only an oblong of green. The land was divided into squares. Those nearby had definite outlines, and a small drainage ditch lay between every two squares. But as you moved away, the ditches and divisions began to disappear until the only thing you saw was a wide stretch of green darkness lit by the myriad lanterns of the yellow cotton flowers.

The line of laborers was visible in the distance, but you could scarcely see it against the dense green which, as you moved farther away, became ever deeper until it shaded at last into total darkness. You would scarcely have known the line was there, if it weren't for the columns of smoke rising from the pits where they burned the blight-stricken cotton leaves.

The donkey, contracting its lungs to bray as hard as it could, wore itself out. But Fikri Afendi, though he never did much reading, because it tired his eyes which were unable to make out the letters very well no matter how near he held the page, was as sharp-eyed as a hawk in the field. Accordingly and despite the braying of his donkey, he observed that the overseers had suddenly risen from their place in the shade behind the laborers and raised their sticks which they brought down with a crack on the laborers' backs or snapped against the cotton branches as their voices came shouting from afar, "Get down lower, boy ... lower, girl!"

That was a piece of play-acting which Fikri Afendi knew well and was tired of seeing repeated. Hardly had his procession arrived on the scene than several of the foremen came running (more of the same old play-acting, in Fikri Afendi's opinion) to win the honor of holding "Mr. Commissioner's" donkey for him as he dismounted.

Pulling his handkerchief out from under the tarboosh and using it to dry his sweaty face and back, Fikri Afendi shouted, "Hey, Arafa!"

Arafa, the head foreman, that is, the migrant workers' boss, and the man who had succeeded in grabbing the donkey's reins this time, as he always did, answered, "Hello, Mr. Commissioner, sir."

The commissioner did not know whether to return the greeting and make it appear the bluff had worked, or ignore it and thereby seem rude. He did neither, since he was there on a mission, and his duty was to carry it out. So that everything would look natural, he must ask Arafa as he always did, "How clean is it?"

"Clean as a whistle, your Commissionership."

Fikri Afendi pretended to ignore his pleasure at the title and eyed him, saying, "And what if I find worm eggs on the cotton?"

Arafa bowed his head and, placing the palm of one hand on his neck, declared, "Then it's my responsibility and my neck."

In a tone that left the other man unsure whether he was joking or serious, Fikri Afendi then said, "To hell with your neck — and to hell with you and your father, too!"

For some reason, Fikri Afendi had the idea that these people really enjoyed having him call them names and curse their fathers. He thought they must feel somehow honored and proud as though he were granting them ranks and titles. They no doubt took such abuse to be tokens of warm friendship and condescension — condescension from him, that is, who was the master of all this property and the absolute ruler of everything it held. At his disposal were more than two thousand *feddans* of the finest soil and everything on them — people, houses, machines, livestock, and crops. He was the sovereign lord of all this, master of the ten overseers, the chief clerk,

26

and the five underclerks, the *ustas*, the guards, the laborers, the peasants, and the farmers. He could honor whomever he pleased, fire whomever he wanted, and slap a fine on anyone he wished. It was in his power to transfer a peasant from one farm to another, to give him land to till or withhold it, and, if he so wanted, to even evict him from the estate forever, and no one would question his decision or dare to oppose him. He could even slap, punch or kick, if he wished. Sometimes he would even arrest someone, sending the accused to the county seat under guard, and his word was law. Fear was the only thing that held him in check, and there were only two things he feared: the inspector, who was his superior, and the owner of the estate. His superior made a tour of inspection once a month, and the owner came every two or three months. And, with the exception of the few hours that they spent on the estate, he was the master *in perpetuum* of all this. Was it any wonder, then, that his abuse of a laborer or a foreman seemed like a favor and an act of condescension?

As a matter of fact, Fikri Afendi was nearly swayed from his purpose by the passing of these thoughts through his mind. Was it right for a man of his great importance to waste his time on something so ridiculous and unworthy? But there he was, and he would lose nothing by his visit, since none of the laborers or foremen knew the real reason for his coming. For a moment he hesitated, but then he found himself saying, "Are the laborers all here, Arafa?"

"Every single one," replied Arafa with enthusiasm.

"Sure?"

"If they aren't, I'll divorce my wife!"

Nonetheless, Fikri Afendi was not convinced. It was his opinion that these people enjoyed an abundant share of very little religion and would swear by all that was holy for a half-piaster's profit. Accordingly, he said, "All right, count them."

"Right away ... your servant," said Arafa.

And, at the top of his lungs, he did just that. Nor, as he counted, did he neglect to demonstrate his zeal in performing his job by cracking his bamboo switch on every bent back within reach in a simulated blow — simulated, that is, since it was unnecessary and therefore meaningless.

Arafa counted the laborers twice. Each time he assured the manager, doubt and fear creeping into his voice, that the number was right and the laborers were all hard at work in the field.

Fikri Afendi was dumbfounded. The boss was speaking the truth. Yet, he was certain one of those laborers was the bastard child's mother. How did that square with their all being there in that long, stooping line? The slut may have forced herself to come to work, but she would not escape him, for the signs of childbirth would give her away, no matter how careful she was. He just had to look them over and try to pick out the worm from their midst — the criminal who gave birth in the night, did away with her child, and then came here to bend her back, work, and take the overseers' blows as if she were not a human being at all but some kind of female demon or saint.

Fikri Afendi stepped into the square in front of the row of laborers, and fighting the sun's glare, paused before each female in silent scrutiny. Ignoring the old women, he stopped in front of those who were middle-aged, and stood for a long time beside the young girls. For the first time in Fikri Afendi's life, he took a good look at how the Gharabwa dressed, and he learned their women wore brightly colored, very long drawers that were ankle-length and had pleated hems.

Fikri Afendi had moved more than halfway down the line of laborers, and not a single woman had given him cause to stop. The line was nearly at an end, and he had not yet found the object of his quest. Then, suddenly he caught sight of something that sent a ray of hope through him — a bent female back. It was the only back that looked like a woman's being narrow at the waist and ending in a broadly prominent posterior. The head, too, was the only one that was obviously female. It wore a colored kerchief revealing an abundant mass of shiny, black hair.

"It must be her," he said to himself. "Get down lower, girl!"

As he spoke the last sentence, he brought down his cane in a mortally cruel blow on the back that was already bent and had no need to bend further. The woman made a sound of pain when the blow fell. Unable to restrain herself, she straightened up and put a hand to her throbbing back, an imploring moan of pain having escaped her. The commissioner stared into the face that was contracted in pain. ...

Healthy and unmarked, her face bore no evidence of sickness or childbirth. The signs of pain visible on her features were recent, caused by the blow from the cane and not the result of bearing a child the night before. The commissioner moved on to another back. From back to back he went, searching, staring, and making sure. When the line of laborers came to an end, Fikri Afendi's rage knew no bounds. He had come out of his survey with nothing, not even a glimmer of hope.

All of a sudden, Fikri Afendi found himself shouting at Arafa, "Get them out of the field! ... Let them walk by me one at a time!"

Arafa froze in temporary stupidity, and did not open his mouth until the commissioner barked at him again.

The laborers appeared overjoyed by the decision to bring them out of the field, since it meant they would rest, if only for a few moments, from the relentless stooping that, sharp and cruel, they maintained for more than ten hours a day. What great joy to relax for even a minute!

The laborers straightened their backs, and, with one accord and without exception, their hands moved to press the painful spots in their backbones. When they recovered from the short trance of delirium that had seized them and learned of the commissioner's order, the women and young girls were greatly delighted. Each one began to indulge in the hope of a thousand-and-one-nights of dreams, believing the commissioner's choice must surely fall upon her and she would spend the pleasantest of hours walking lightly and proudly as a maid in his house, carrying dishes or passing the water jug where a person could sit and there was plenty of food and shade, and sticks, canes, and foremen did not exist. Meanwhile, the men passed by with the indifference of those sentenced to a long term in prison. ...

The laborers filed past the commissioner as Fikri Afendi looked hard at their faces ... old and young ... wrinkled and smooth ... ugly and pretty ... stupid and sick. He also studied their bodies: slender and stooped, limping and sprightly, withered and blooming, bodies that were saying farewell to life, and others, ushering it in. Among all those faces and bodies, he was unable to find one that belonged to that wicked, criminal mother.

Fikri Afendi shouted to Arafa to return the laborers to the field as he damned their fathers and Arafa's, too, this time in spiteful earnest.

As he placed his foot in the stirrup and prepared for the leap that would lift him onto the donkey's back, he racked his brains over two impossibilities.

For, it was impossible that the bastard's mother was anyone but a migrant woman.

And it was just as impossible that she was one of the laborers he had examined.

CHAPTER EIGHT

On the commissioner's way back to the farm, he took the route he had traveled before. Usta Muhammad was still there. Enjoying himself, the old man sat dangling his legs in the water, playing in it with his feet like a child. But when he saw the procession come into sight in the distance, he got to his feet as though stung, and hurried to join it. He did not need to ask to know that failure was the commissioner's companion. For a time he kept quiet as he panted along with the others, avoiding the clouds of dust; then he spoke up in his elderly and enthusiastic stammer, "Mr. Commissioner, d-d-do what the Caliph Omar d-d-did."

In moments of despair people grab at straws. Fikri Afendi pulled on the reins of his mount a little to make it slow down. When Usta Muhammad was running beside him, he asked, "What did he do, you old fool?"

The story that the old *usta* told was long, and lasted until they got all the way back to the big farm. It began with the Caliph Omar traveling incognito through the city of Medina to see how his subjects fared. During his travels, he came upon the corpse of a young man who had been stabbed with a dagger. The caliph tried to find the murderer, but in vain. When he finally despaired, a wise old man said to him, "If you want to find the murderer, wait nine months, and you'll have him." The caliph did not take what the old man said seriously. Exactly nine months later, however, a rumor spread throughout Medina that so-and-so's daughter had had a child out of wedlock. Then the old man said to the caliph, "There's your killer. ... The woman who had the baby must be the murderess." "How can that be?" asked the caliph. In answer, the wise man said, "No doubt he attacked her, and so she killed him."

The story appealed to Fikri Afendi and nearly succeeded in cheering him up, but it had nothing to do with the present situation. It was just another one of Usta Muhammad's many stories that he made up for all occasions as though the problems of the world could be solved through fairy tales.

All that happened was that he had given up hope of satisfying his curiosity and finding the foundling's mother, and he made up his mind to forget the matter entirely, and notify the county authorities. Let them do what they liked. As an added precaution, he dictated the report to the chief clerk, Mesiha Afendi, choosing his words with painstaking care so that he and the estate would be cleared of all responsibility.

And the police arrived.

The prosecuting attorney came, too.

As did the health inspector.

The administration buildings were vacated for them, and the prosecuting attorney took over the commissioner's office. Policemen, smoking narghiles and sipping tea, stood here and there around the building, and a man who was obviously a detective loitered near Junaidi's store. Meanwhile, the people of the estate stationed themselves some distance away to watch what went on, start rumors, and whisper among themselves.

Commissioner Fikri Afendi was busy, in truth, because he had decided to take advantage of the opportunity and prepare a lavish banquet for the men of supreme authority in the county. He had many interests to promote, and it was rare that such men came to the estate. Accordingly, he covered the distance between his house, which lay at the verge of the big farm, and the administration buildings dozens of times personally to supervise the turkey, and to taste the bread that was prepared in his house especially for the banquet. As he went in and out of the administration buildings, the farm residents regarding him in wonder, he felt an unbounded happiness, because he alone had the right to speak with the police commissioner, the prosecuting attorney, and the health inspector.

And the investigation began. ...

Each migrant woman was called in, having first been kicked several times so she would be afraid, and confess. Nabawiya was brought in, too, clutching her basket of eggs, which she did not want to leave when, as she said, it held all her capital. Abd al-Muttalib and old Usta Muhammad were questioned, as well.

And the investigation ended. It was established that the foundling was strangled, and the crime charged to a person or persons unknown. The prosecution gave permission for the small corpse to be buried in the estate cemetery, and Abd al-Muttalib volunteered to take care of the shrouding and burial.

The men of supreme authority ate their lunch, and said good-bye.

The day ended.

CHAPTER NINE

As the day ended, the estate — administration, peasants and employees — gave itself up to an even greater sense of bewilderment. For, no sooner had they heard about the foundling than they relaxed and said, "It's those migrants." But now the facts had proven otherwise: the migrants were innocent. Even Commissioner Fikri Afendi, who had insisted the culprit was a migrant, began to sound a little doubtful. And yet every time he saw the migrant laborers going to or from the field, his eyes would search, involuntarily and in spite of himself, for the women in their midst — maybe suddenly he would see signs of depravity, the forbidden. At first he was jumpy and out-of-sorts, but as the days passed, strange impulses began to stir within him whenever he saw a migrant woman. And one day he even found he was joking with one of them. Another time he pretended to himself and to everyone else that he poked a girl in the bosom to scold her. It was natural that his hand should bump her breasts, and he was a little startled to find them virginal, hard and firm like an inflated rubber ball. He was astonished to see the girl's face grow pale all of a sudden as though drained of blood. Then at once her color deepened, her cheeks flushing, and she gave a start as though embarrassed or angry. ... Good Lord! Was it possible for migrant women to feel anger or shame?!

The matter did not pass quite so easily, however, for the rest of the estate's inhabitants. It was as though a huge rock had been thrown into brackish, stagnant water. Doubts and accusations began to rain down from every direction until not a farm woman remained who was safe from suspicion, even though they all knew their women were innocent. But every sin has a sinner, and every crime, a criminal. This crime was no exception. They knew exactly what the crime was; but who was responsible?

What was more, suspicion began to creep from the lowly houses of the peasants to the lofty ones of the employees. Mesiha Afendi, the chief clerk, began to have certain doubts, and to fear the forbidden had happened. To be truthful, he always feared it would, living as he did in constant fear of everything.

Mesiha Afendi was the most firmly established employee on the estate, having been raised there in the princess's day. He had risen gradually from being a hired laborer whose father sent him to learn the three R's from Master Qaysar, the old chief clerk and high priest of bookkeeping, who understood all its secrets and hidden lore. And so, sent by his father, Mesiha sat at Master Qaysar's feet in mingled dread and admiration, waiting like a faithful dog for his teacher now and then to throw him a sum which he would snatch up, heart pounding, frightened to death he would solve it wrong and anger the chief clerk who would retaliate by keeping the secrets of the trade from him. For this reason, Mesiha was at Master Qaysar's beck and call: waiting on him in his house, shopping for him in the far-off city, and guarding his bottle of raisin liquor with his life. When Master Qaysar cleared his throat to speak, Mesiha's ears would open wide, and when the old man said something, Mesiha would not just listen, but more accurately, would stretch out hidden fingers from his ears to seize each word coming from his mouth, and slip it quickly into his head, fearful it would be lost or wasted. After all, it was through the chief clerk's words and bookkeeping that Mesiha was to move from one class to another, and make the transition from being a young man fated to farm and work with a hoe to being a gentleman — an *afendi* — sitting at a desk and wielding that small, magical object: the pen.

Every word that Master Qaysar spoke stayed in his brain, saturating it like a pure and indelible dye — every single word, even the anecdotes he told. The most important of these stories was one he related on a certain evening, for it was to become the compass of Mesiha's life. Master Qaysar had asked him, "How much is two times two, Mesiha, my son?" Like a clever pupil, Mesiha had answered, "Four, sir."

To his surprise, the teacher replied, "Ah-h-h. ... You'll never be a chief clerk, Mesiha." Saddened and distressed, Mesiha asked his teacher why not, and he told him the following story: Once upon a time there was a landowner who wanted to hire a clerk. He advertised an opening, and men seeking the position began to arrive from all over the world. Meeting with them one at a time, the landowner did not question them about their qualifications, their names or where they had worked before, but only asked them that question which Mesiha had been asked, "How much is two times two?"

Every time he asked that question, and was given the immediate response, "Four," he told the jobseeker, "Get out." This went on until one day an elderly man arrived, carrying a ledger under his arm, and holding in his hand a pouch with an inkwell and quill pen (as was the custom in writing long ago). When the man stood before the landowner, he was asked the usual question, "How much is two times two?" "Two times two?" asked the man. "That's right," said the landowner. Then the man said to him, "Wait just one moment, sir. Yes, sir, I'll tell you."

Sitting down, he opened the ledger that was with him, took out the inkwell and quill pen, and wrote on the paper before him: 2 x 2 = 4. Then he told the landowner, "Yes, sir. Two times two is four, barring all negligence and error."

At once the landowner said, "Enough. The position is yours. Congratulations. ..." Caution, prudence, and leaving nothing to chance were what Master Qaysar taught him. Those were the things that enabled him to succeed the old man in his position when he died, and to work on the estate for more than forty years in accordance with that rule, without negligence or error. Commissioners and inspectors came and went, the land was bought and sold, and he alone remained eternally constant, sitting behind his big desk, surrounded by piles of ledgers, the least of which weighed twenty pounds. He was the authority on the history and affairs of the estate, he knew every peasant by name and by parentage, and he remembered the loan that so-and-so took out before even opening the ledger. Yet, in spite of his long association with the peasants, he treated them with the utmost reserve. Although he mixed with them, laughed with them, and was consulted by them about their most personal affairs, he always remained Mesiha Afendi, the chief clerk.

The foundling awoke Mesiha Afendi's suspicions, because he was the best-informed person on the estate when it came to the rumors that circulated there, especially the ones concerning himself and his family. Mesiha Afendi had three sons. Two were in high school, while the third and oldest had graduated, and, thanks to his father's efforts, worked as a clerk on a nearby farm. The chief clerk had a daughter, too. He made her finish elementary school, and then he kept her at home to await her bridegroom. But there were not many suitors, since where would they learn about the young lady who sat waiting for them in that faraway place to the north? Even her being the most beautiful girl on the estate did not intercede in her behalf. For, compared to the peasant girls, Linda was as white as carded cotton. Her coloring by itself was enough to make her a beauty queen, although when she and her mother traveled to Cairo to visit their relatives in Shubra, her mother would hear with her own ears the relatives and neighbor women whisper that Linda's nose was too big, her mouth a little too wide, her figure not slim enough, and her hair coarse and kinky.

That, however, was in Cairo's Shubra. On the estate Linda was the unrivaled beauty. She was so beautiful that the heart of every young peasant pounded with emotion when he caught a distant glimpse of her looking down from the window of her house, or walking along the canal with her family and the family of the commissioner.

It was the commissioner's family that was the source of the problem. His wife, Umm Safwat, was a peasant woman, or that was what she seemed when she talked to Afifa, the chief clerk's wife, who was brought up in Cairo, and who was educated, and used to city ways. Because Umm Safwat was the boss's wife, Afifa was forever embarrassing her, and showing up her backwardness and ignorance. And she did this with all the subtlety of Shubra and the caution of her husband Mesiha. Umm Safwat would become enraged, and giving in to reckless defiance, she would spend long hours cursing and slandering Afifa in front of the peasant women.

Actually, the commissioner and his family were not the source of the problem. It was really his only son Safwat. He was twenty years old, had failed his high school finals for the third time, and was spoiled and indulged by his parents, the peasants, and everyone on the estate. All day long, a shotgun slung on his shoulder, dressed like a dandy in a white, peasant-style *gallabiya*, and wearing a yellow hat and sunglasses, he would hunt pigeons. Pigeon hunting was the only thing Safwat liked, and the only place he liked to hunt was by the canal that passed in front of the chief clerk's house. Everyone knew why. For years people had talked about the hunter and the pigeons, Mr. Safwat and Miss Linda, and the burning passion kept under control by the canal, lack of opportunity, and difference of religion. It was kept imprisoned in Safwat's heart, and Linda's especially, was locked tight against it. Sometimes, however, it appeared in the way she lifted her arm as though to hold onto the window grating when what she meant instead was a shy, hidden greeting, or in a picture they said Linda kept in the heart-shaped gold locket that hung from her marble-white neck, or in letters it was claimed they exchanged through Mahboob.

Mahboob was the mailman on the estate, since there was no post office. He was the one who went to the Delta train station located at the edge of the estate, and when the small train came rolling in, he would climb into the mail window to give the employee the official and personal letters he had, and receive the incoming mail. Mahboob was very short. He was barely as tall as a child, and perhaps that was why he was always one jump ahead of people, and never seemed to tire of making jokes at his own expense. He was short, his features were tiny, and his legs were no longer than the span of your hand. Even the bag in which he carried the mail was small, its leather as creased and faded as his face.

He was, at the same time, the strangest mailman, since he could neither read nor write. In spite of this and because of the small number of people on the estate who got mail, he knew from long experience that the letter coming from al-Mansuura was for the commissioner, and that the one from al-Gaafariya, written in copying pencil with the slanted handwriting, was for Sheikh Shaabaan from his relative there. That was how Mahboob distributed the mail. He gave the official letters to Mesiha Afendi, and handed out the rest to their recipients without making a single mistake.

Mahboob was married to Zakiya, one of the tallest and heaviest women on the estate. When the men had nothing better to do, they would tie up Mahboob, and try to make him confess how he slept with her, laughing as he begged for mercy. But strangest of all, Zakiya, unlike her husband, knew how to read and write very well. She was the only woman on the estate who could read the newspaper. The one newspaper that came to the estate was the *Muqattam*. Why the *Muqattam,* in particular, no one knew. Maybe it was because the administration in Cairo subscribed to it. Or perhaps it was because the *Muqattam* devoted more space to agricultural news than any other newspaper. Then again it might have been because it, like the estate, was owned by foreigners.

Zakiya was addicted to reading the newspaper. She would even block her husband's way when he came from the station, and force him off his donkey to get hold of it. Nor would she relinquish the paper until she had devoured it completely. Mahboob, standing there helpless, would be more afraid of her than of being late for the commissioner. He could always blame the delay on the Delta train, which did not have a fixed schedule. But there was no way he could talk his way past Zakiya. How could he when the farm where they lived was on the way to the big farm and the administration, and she was always waiting to ambush him?

They said, then, that Safwat and Linda exchanged letters by way of Mahboob. Linda would give him a letter, and instead of taking it to the Delta train, he would rush it to the place where the shots from Safwat's gun could be heard echoing, even if that were at the very end of the estate. And there he would be rewarded with sweets, a pigeon or two, and a tip.

Mesiha Afendi was aware of all this. Many times he stopped Mahboob and searched him, pretending to be looking for a letter, but never once did he find anything in Mahboob's bag, or even in his pockets when he insisted on searching them.

Yes, today, in the wake of this strange event, Mesiha Afendi's suspicions were aroused. Although it wasn't time for him to leave the office (there were no set working hours, but he usually stayed until lunchtime), on that day he rose and left the office building, crossed the stone bridge, and headed toward his house which stood at the verge of the farm, receiving the greetings of the peasants with a grunt. In spite of his preoccupation, he did not forget to gather up the hem of his long *gallabiya,* holding it off the ground for fear the dirt on the road would soil it. He was dressed as usual: a white, collarless, shirt-style robe, a white coat, and a tarboosh; everything was white, but you couldn't see a single spot. Often Umm Safwat scolded her husband the commissioner when he came home with his yellow trousers dirty, the cuffs full of clay, pebbles, and dirt. She would lecture him and say he was not worth the nail cuttings of Mesiha Afendi whom she had never seen with a speck of dirt on his clothing. Mesiha Afendi took such extremely good care of his wardrobe that, when he went traveling and was absolutely forced to wear the one suit that he owned (which always looked as new as though he bought it this year even though it was by no means less than ten years old), he would put two handkerchiefs inside the collar, fearing the sweat from the back of his neck would seep through if he satisfied himself with only one.

With his short, stooped frame and pale face (he was the only man on the estate who spent most of the day working indoors), heavy beard, and spotless clothing held well off the ground, Mesiha Afendi climbed the few steps that led to the door of his house. The door was open — there being but few occasions when you shut the doors of houses in the country — and he went in. Mesiha Afendi usually created quite a stir when he came home. As soon as he set foot on the threshold, his questions and comments would start: "He-e-ey. ... Where are you? ... What are you doing? ... I sent you the vegetables with the boy. ... How come you're late with lunch? ... Was the meat tough? ... This is fine. ... What's the matter with you, Linda? ... Have you got a toothache or what? ..."

As he said this, he would shake his head like someone hunting for something with his nose, his gray eyes boring everywhere. This time, however, he entered the house silently, gloomily. In the sitting room (which was lighted more than was necessary) sat his wife Afifa, a low, round table in front of her. With her were her brother-in-law Dumyaan, and Umm Ibrahim, wife of the estate's Quran-reciter. The three were engaged in making vermicelli. Dumyaan held the dough, and as he twisted it with one hand, he read Umm Ibrahim's fortune in her coffee cup with the other, telling her, "You'll have good luck after 'two dots.'* Be patient."

Mesiha Afendi nearly scolded his brother, and that, too, was unusual. He knew, as did everyone else, that his brother was feeble-minded, his brain apparently having stopped developing when he was a child. For, although his body, which was short and slight like his brother's, grew to be that of a man in his thirty-fifth year, and he had a thick, black beard like a clothesbrush which he shaved only once in a while, his mind was that of a ten-year-old child. ... He never changed out of his cashmere *gallabiya*, and he never removed the brimmed skullcap that was made of the same material. His job was to work in his brother's house, and there he cleaned the copper, measured the chickens,** and taught the young chicks' legs not to stray with the neighbors' fowl. He washed the clothes, and brought things from the store, watched the children, and shined their shoes. And he did all this while living in a childish kingdom of his own creation. When he met you in the middle of the road and you said, "How are you, Khawaaga*** Dumyaan?", he would stop you, saying, "God keep you from harm." Then he would lift his face to the sky as

---

*Turkish coffee grounds are used to tell fortunes as follows: after the coffee has been drunk, a thick layer of grounds is left in the bottom of the cup which is then turned over onto its saucer and slowly rotated. The grounds are allowed to dry, forming a pattern which the fortuneteller reads. The "two dots" mentioned in the story refer to a time interval (e.g., two days, two weeks, etc.) whose exact length is interpreted according to the distribution of the grounds. For example, the closer together the dots are in the pattern, the shorter the time interval — Tr.

**This is a task usually given to servants and young girls which involves inserting a probe into the hen's oviduct to determine if it will lay an egg the following day. The fact that Dumyaan was assigned this menial chore reveals much about his status in his brother's household — Tr.

***The word *khawaaga* is a title or form of address used for Western Christians which approximates "sir" or "Mr." — Tr.

if reading what fate had in store for you, and wetting his index finger and thumb, he would lay them across the back of his left hand. Holding them up, he would tell you, "God willing, you'll be happy." He was a big toy for the children, a little toy for the men, and a masculine toy for the women.

As far as the women were concerned, they (and sometimes the men) were interested in one thing only, and that was whether Dumyaan was any good with women. Some said Afifa hid nothing from him, and treated him like a young eunuch. Others insisted, "No, his thick, black beard proves his manhood." They would ask, "Dumyaan, why don't you get married?" And laughing in the strange way he had that sounded like a man trying to imitate a child, he would say, "God bless you." Some even went so far in making fun of him they would ask him to convert to Islam, to which he would reply, "I am a Muslim, and I believe in one God," and recite the first chapter of the Quran and the Throne-verse. Others, however, said Dumyaan was a malicious pretender. What made everything so awkward was that Dumyaan was the brother of Mesiha Afendi, the chief clerk. To make fun of the chief clerk's brother was embarrassing — or sometimes gratifying, as though the peasants enjoyed ridiculing the administration to its face when they mocked Dumyaan.

Mesiha Afendi peered into the sitting room and the open room nearby, but he saw no sign of Linda. When he finally saw no other way out, he asked his wife about her, and she said, "She's not feeling well. ..." As though startled, he flew at her, "Why not? ... What's wrong with her? ... Why didn't you tell me? ... What sort of women are these, anyway? ... Where is she? ...

Afifa said she was lying down on their bed. With his rolling gait, Mesiha Afendi arrived at the bedroom. Shabby and extremely ancient, it held the same set of furniture that Afifa brought with her on their wedding day many years ago: a wardrobe without doors, and a bed whose slats had been renewed many times, its posts covered with a thick coating made up of the remains of hardened, black fly eggs, and mosquito netting which was hanging from only three sides, as it was cut off on the fourth. The netting was lowered, and before he even raised it, he said, his suspicions growing, "What's wrong, Linda? ..."

He found her sleeping. He thought she was pretending, and his heart grew more troubled. Raising the netting, he confronted her. Her curly, yellow hair (which no one ever saw unless it was elegantly arranged and cared for as if its owner instinctively knew how coarse it was and constantly tried to make it seem smooth and silky) was disheveled. A lock of it covered her forehead, and her eyes were a little swollen as if she had been crying.

Her father asked what was wrong, and she told him her stomach hurt. For some reason, perhaps the way she said it, or perhaps the sight of her, hair uncombed and eyes swollen and puffy-lidded, for some reason, Mesiha Afendi felt, suddenly and unequivocally, that his daughter Linda must be responsible for the morning's crime. So strong was the feeling that it made him stop talking and stare at her as though she were not the girl he was used to seeing as his daughter, as though she were a stranger and could be the immoral wanton who had committed the morning's crime. Caught between this suspicion and the certainty that she was his darling, precious daughter Linda, Mesiha Afendi began to examine her with his narrow eyes, and to touch her hand and stomach, pretending to be asking about what bothered her, especially her stomach. It was not as yielding as a new mother's would be, but it did hurt her.

Mesiha Afendi distrusted only those others, the peasants, commissioners, administration, and so on. He had never doubted himself or anyone under his control ... his family ... especially his daughter Linda. Her life was an open book for him, her mother, and everyone. Even the rumor about the messages she and Safwat exchanged with their eyes, and the looks and gestures that passed between them was hardly a secret. And this, her public life, was her whole existence. Was it possible she had another life — one that she pursued in the darkness with Safwat, the commissioner's son? Would that the matter came in the form of bewildered questions wanting an answer! Instead, it came upon Mesiha like a fever that overwhelmed him without his being able to speak or give vent to his emotions. Linda's stomach-ache might be real, or it might be a pretense, a protective screen. His wife Afifa might be as he had always known her, full of idle talk and chatter but the loyal and trustworthy companion of his life. Then again, she might not be. She might be the one shielding her daughter. For all he knew, she might even be protecting herself. ...

Mesiha Afendi could no longer stay in the room. He felt suffocated, and was unable to remain there any longer. He left the bedroom for the sitting room and its occupants gathered around the vermicelli. Afifa noticed the change in his expression, and asked what was wrong. He hemmed and hawed, and she understood nothing of what he said. Calling to Dumyaan to follow him, Mesiha left the house, walking slowly to let the other catch up. The canal bridge stretched in front of the house then witnessed the strangest dialogue occur between the two brothers. It was blisteringly hot, and the sun was at its zenith, its millions of ovens blasting forth hot lava upon the universe. As Mesiha Afendi walked with Dumyaan beside him, he tried, for the first time in his life, to have a serious conversation with him, a conversation such as two brothers might have. He tried to ask him if he had seen anything, or if anything had come to his attention; he asked him about Safwat and Linda, and about the forbidden. Meanwhile, Dumyaan was heedlessly launched on a strange tale about a hen. Every day he would measure the bird and find it about to lay, but the hen never produced anything. He was sure there was something secret about the egg, and that it might even hold the key to treasure. He was afraid to kill the bird and lose the secret and the treasure, but he was just as afraid to let it live and have the neighbors steal it.

At last Mesiha Afendi could stand it no longer. He scolded his brother and, cursing violently, left him. Dumyaan stood bewildered for some time, having paused in his ramblings. But it was not long before he realized that his brother had cursed him for what would seem to have been the first time, since he soon began to cry like an unjustly treated child. He took off his skullcap to dry his tears, and his head appeared, bald and gleaming, to strike sparks beneath the sun.

CHAPTER TEN

At the same time, the commissioner's son Safwat, all but in a stupor, was lying propped against the armrest of the only couch in the house of Ahmad Sultan, the estate's personnel clerk. That was Safwat's favorite way — and place — to sit. When Ahmad got through with work, he would go home, and the two of them would relax — sometimes with a narghile, sometimes with a woman, and sometimes with a cup of coffee.* Ahmad Sultan was the only bachelor among the estate employees. He was also the only employee who, in his house right next door to Mesiha Afendi's, lived by himself. And Ahmad Sultan was the only employee who was close to Safwat's heart. Both of them were young, and more importantly, Ahmad was older than Safwat, more experienced, and had a surer knowledge of what went on within the houses on the estate. Yet, it was not friendship in the usual sense that drew them together, for Ahmad Sultan never forgot to treat Safwat as the son of the commissioner who was his boss and who ran the estate. Likewise, there was a certain measure of reserve in Safwat's behavior toward Ahmad who was just barely able to read and write — God only knew how he had made it to his position. What a difference there was between him and Safwat who was getting ready to enter the university and finish his education in Cairo. Nonetheless — despite all these considerations — theirs was a model friendship. It was also the cause of much distress for Commissioner Fikri Afendi who trusted Ahmad Sultan not at all. But neither scoldings nor even violent arguments with his son were successful in severing the relationship.

Safwat leaned back against the armrest of the couch as he and Ahmad exchanged a "loaded" cigarette. They took turns dragging on it, at the same time being careful to keep the ash from falling as though they'd lose the mood if it did. A conversation was going on,

---

*Although a cup of coffee sounds innocuous enough, the author means a cup that was "doped" with hashish or opium — Tr.

and it naturally revolved around the foundling, the most important news item of the day.

Actually, it was not a conversation in the usual sense. Safwat was at the high point of his desire to know Ahmad Sultan's connection with the foundling as though the relationship had been proven in front of him, and all he had to do was find out exactly what it was. He did not, however, want to appear like a curious child in the eyes of Ahmad Sultan. He wanted to make him believe that his questions were what one experienced man asked another. Perhaps that was why he sat on the couch the way he did, propped up on an elbow with the air of a sophisticated, sharp-witted man of the world. It may also have been the reason for that smile of his which was meant to say, "I know just what you've been up to." Even the way he stroked his moustache (his pale moustache which, no more than a year old, was carefully cultivated to look much older) was done with deliberation as though it were an adult caress for a grown-up moustache.

Ahmad Sultan listened, a big grin not leaving his features. In the presence of that smile, Safwat always felt that, no matter how much he talked about his adventures, he was young and nothing more than a failing pupil in the school of principal Ahmad Sultan. He assumed it was a smile of mockery and derision, but it might not have been.

Safwat went on talking with Ahmad Sultan listening until it seemed Safwat had at last exhausted his bag of tricks, since he said, "Abu Hamid. ... Honestly, whose kid is it?"

Here Ahmad gave a shout of laughter, one of those loud laughs of his that could be heard in Mesiha Afendi's house. Every time Mesiha heard Sultan's laughter as it penetrated the walls and reached his ears, nearly splitting them, he would shudder, screw up his face, and let fly with a word of abuse. For some reason, Safwat did not trust Sultan's laughter, thinking that it, too, was sarcastic. That may have been why he went on to say, "You know, you're very deep. Aren't you?"

His laughter reverting to a smile, Ahmad asked, "Why?"

Safwat proceeded to explain why he was deep and sly, for how could he let himself have adventures and not tell Safwat when together the two of them had gone through thick and thin?

Ahmad tried to change the subject by asking Safwat for the latest news about Linda. To be frank, that was Safwat's favorite topic. He never grew tired of talking about it, and no session with Ahmad Sultan went by without its being mentioned. For, in spite of everything — the hunting rifle slung on his shoulder, his adventures in Cairo and the provincial capital, and his brief relationships with some of the women on the estate—, Linda occupied a special place in his heart in which she dwelled constantly. He had not met her often, and the sentences that had passed between them in conversation during the long years of their two families' acquaintance could be counted on the fingers of one hand. But there was a certain something he felt inside toward her, and he sensed it, too, in the way she looked at him. Although this something was unspoken and unseen, it was most definitely there, and it provided him with a secret sorrow that thrilled his inner feelings and made him, whenever he felt it, want to break down and cry, or laugh, or tear down the mansion and all the other estate buildings. Sometimes when he strolled along the canal that faced Mesiha Afendi's house, he would find Linda standing at the window, remote, her face purely shining, encircled by the window's dark halo. When he saw her like that, he felt a strange current flowing within him that made him want to fly and sing, or just stand where he was and do nothing for the rest of his life but steal glances at her now and then to find her looking his way, or at least, in the direction of the canal. And oh, if he raised his gun in the air and then shifted it from one shoulder to another, trying to make the movement a sign of greeting, and she lifted her right hand and raised it to grasp the window grille from above as though she returned his salute, then, the earth shook under him, and all through the day and every night he went on remembering that moment. He would slowly replay the movement in his mind's eye, shaken by an excitement that transported him far away from the world, his family, and the estate in an intoxicating trance from which he did not want to wake.

With Ahmad Sultan, the hiding place of his secret, and in his bedroom that was practically void of furnishings Safwat would let himself go and narrate the details of his love, whenever there was anything to tell. And always the session would end with that perplexed question: did Ahmad think Linda loved him?

Every time he asked Ahmad this question, he would assure him she did. But it was not his assurance that was important, but the smile with which he gave it. If he would only once answer him without smiling, he would truly believe his words were sincere.

It was appropriate that Safwat respond to the opening Ahmad had given him, and become engrossed in the subject of Linda. Today, however, that was not Safwat's goal. He wanted to know about his friend's exploits, or at least, the one that could have led to the foundling.

It would appear that Safwat's perseverance had its effect. For, after two cigarettes, Ahmad Sultan's tongue was loosened, and he proceeded to talk, or rather, to confess. He began by telling Safwat, "You know Hagg Badawi's wife and daughter?"

"Uh-huh," said Safwat.

Continuing, Ahmad Sultan declared, "I swear that one of them was here in the room with me on that very bed while the other was hiding up on the roof. ... You know the girl who worked with the laborers separating the cotton — the silly one?"

"Which one?" asked Safwat.

"The tall one who acted so young and stupid."

"Oh-h-h. ..."

"Believe me, she told me herself to take her."

"And did you?"

"What should I have done — embarrassed her, Mister Safwat?!"

Ahmad Sultan's room that evening was witness to tales that nearly made Safwat's hair stand on end, tales that had him believing that, with all his adventures and all he had done, he was no more than a drop in the ocean of Ahmad Sultan. Things did not stop there, however, nor did Ahmad Sultan's confessions end with himself, but went far beyond, and — word by word, and truth by truth — laid bare the other side of life on the estate, the side that was always hidden and never came to light, the side that no one ever saw — snarled and entangled, and full of what seemed stranger than anyone could imagine — intimate relations between sons and their fathers' wives, liaisons between virtuous women and immoral men, and between immoral women and virtuous men, relationships between day laborers and people so pious they had gone on the pilgrimage to Mecca — even the history of the dead found its way into the room.

At last and after a lengthy introduction which Safwat cited to prove he was neutral and wanted only to know, regardless of his personal involvement, Safwat broached the subject for whose sake he had sat and taken such a long time to sound the situation out. He asked Ahmad Sultan, making him swear by everything that was sacred, to tell the truth. He asked him what he knew about the other side of Linda.

And this time, with a serious expression that did not tolerate doubts about his sincerity, Ahmad Sultan denied that he knew anything shameful about her. Safwat insisted on asking him again, and again Ahmad persisted in his denial.

Nonetheless, when Safwat rose in preparation for going home as

45

the sun, too, got ready to set, he was still not completely convinced.

*   *   *

Ahmad Sultan stayed seated in the same rattan chair with the armrests for a long time, staring at the ceiling and out the room's only window, lost in thought. Then, a strange gleam began to steal its way into his eyes, a gleam like the glitter of madness or the bright flash of ecstasy. As if baffled by some great problem, he began to stir uneasily in his chair. His restlessness did not last long, however, for soon he rose and left the house. He spent some time walking cautiously up and down the main street of the farm, although since he was the only person in the administration to break the rule of employees not associating with peasants, his presence in the middle of the street or in one of the houses provoked neither surprise nor inquiry. At an open door he paused briefly, and with a flick of his robe and a movement of his hand, the woman who sat inside understood he wanted her to meet him at the mosque.

The mosque was located at the farm's western corner. Cheaply built of sun-dried bricks, it had a short minaret that looked like a raised, truncated finger. The road to the mosque was deserted most of the time, since it was seldom used except for the Friday prayers. The peasants performed the rest of their religious duties in a prayer-place that stood by the canal. At first it was located near the big canal facing the house where the commissioner lived, but he ordered them to stop using it and then had it torn down, building the other in its stead. The sight of the peasants sitting in the prayer-place right in front of his home — "invading the privacy" of the house and its inhabitants as he put it — aggravated him to the point of fury. It was even worse when they arrived in the early morning, and stripped off their clothes to dive in the canal for ablutions. ...

Ahmad Sultan did not have to pace back and forth behind the mosque for very long before the flowing, black dress whose owner he knew appeared to him from out of the twilight. It was Umm Ibrahim, the wife of the estate's Quran-reciter, who was in every way a remarkable woman from the manner in which she painted her eyelids with kohl and tightly stretched a kerchief across her forehead to the way she held the skirt of her long dress with one hand, and lightly swung the other in time to her graceful, swaying walk.

She was very well acquainted with Ahmad Sultan, since she was one of the first women he knew when he came to the estate. Later their liaison developed into a kind of friendship. She cooked for him on occasion, and sometimes gave him a dish of homemade cream, even though she had lost hope of ever renewing their relationship.

46

Ahmad Sultan greeted her warmly and pinched her belly just like old times. And, after a long scolding from her and a string of excuses from himself, he said, "I need you for something."

"Just name it. ..."

"Linda!"

He said the one word and was silent. She did not question him, waiting for him to finish, and fearing at the same time he would not. She understood and he understood, and there was no need for either of them to pretend otherwise.

After a pause during which she studied his good-looking face and his smile, she spoke. "But she's too hard, I couldn't. ..."

With a sound of exasperation, Ahmad pinched her in the belly again. Arching her body to move her stomach away and bring her face closer to his, she tried to dissuade him. But she knew her attempt would fail. For, anytime he made up his mind to have something, it was his, and anything he said to her was nothing but an order which she must obey.

She was silent for some time. Then her features relaxed a little, and smiling, she raised her index finger and pointed first at her right eye and then at her left as though saying, "I promise."

It was at that moment that a hoarse, raucous voice calling the faithful to evening prayers came to them from a distance, the voice of Abu Ibrahim, her husband. Even though the man himself was far away in the prayer-place, the sound of his voice ended their meeting at once. Umm Ibrahim turned and went back, her slippers clicking, as though Abu Ibrahim's voice had caught her in the act. Ahmad Sultan, however, took his time in leaving. Gazing at the farm with its few, scattered lights, he inhaled the aroma of rice, fish, and onions as it mixed with the heavy odor of smoke. As he contemplated the vast, encompassing night, he dreamt of Linda and the evening she would come in fear and trembling to his house and *the* room, and of how he would bring pleasure to her loneliness and, with his miraculous power, transform her shyness into boldness, coquetry, and daring.

CHAPTER ELEVEN

Supper took longer than usual that evening, and the short get-together of the men that followed it lasted late into the night. Junaidi kept his store open and his kerosene pressure lamp burning until after ten o'clock while the men sat in a long row on the wall of the stone bridge. They could talk of nothing but the foundling.

It wasn't only the big farm that buzzed with talk. The news traveled, as well, to neighboring farms and even nearby villages, carried there by people who lived in them, and worked on the estate. The event was truly momentous, for life on the estate was easygoing without anything to disturb its order but an occasional quarrel or a petty theft. But the finding of a murdered baby one morning, well, that was reason enough to convene councils and not adjourn them, since it was something that people could debate forever.

The people who inhabited the estate were clever with words. They were natural-born talkers, famous for their skill. People even said the reason for it was fish, which was the principal fare of practically everyone living on the estate and in the general area. They were experts at telling stories and highlighting details, and could skillfully produce elaborate lists of excuses. Even their pronunciation of words — owing to how much they talked — was clear and unambiguous. For the people of the estate, conversation was a hobby, practically their only one, and there were people of genius among them, people who, when they went to a meeting, naturally took a front seat, having the glibbest tongues around. There were many with such talents. Usta Muhammad was one, as was Muhammad Abu Tulba, and the granddaddy of them all was Sheikh Abd al-Waarith al-Kabir. Sheikh Abd al-Waarith was skilled not only at talking, but also at farming. Farming is a craft, and there are skilled farmers, lazy ones, rich farmers and clever ones, farmers who decide for themselves when to irrigate, and others who water their land only because their neighbor does. Sheikh Abd al-Waarith was just about the cleverest person on the estate when it came to farming. You could even say he was practically the peasants' permanent consultant in cases where problems with the land had driven them to their wits' end. With his moustache that was neither thick nor thin, spotless turban, dark complexion and confident, brown eyes, he was the one whose slow and soothing speech had the final say in any argument that arose. Even the commissioner did not proceed with important estate matters such as when to plant rice, or plow and level the wheatfield to make it ready for corn until he had first consulted Sheikh Abd al-Waarith, since his opinion was always superior to that of the overseers and important peasants who also advised him.

Sheikh Abd al-Waarith was presiding over the men who sat in front of Junaidi's store, and for what seemed to be the first time he was without an opinion. Every time the men's ideas clashed and differed, and they looked searchingly at him, waiting for him to speak up, he did nothing more than clear his throat self-consciously and say, "God alone knows best, men."

He did not even stay with them for long, since soon he excused himself and rose, claiming he hadn't yet prayed that evening and must do so before sleep took him unawares.

The men who went on sitting there, just like their sleepless fellows at the bridge or inside the houses, remained perplexed. The Gharabwa appeared to be innocent of the charge, and no woman or young girl on the farm was left whose behavior had not been discussed and everyone convinced she was not the culprit. Nothing remained but that the foundling came from a neighboring farm or village. But the question was: why would anyone go through the rigors of a long, arduous trip to dispose of the baby when he or she could have left it somewhere in the middle of a field?

There were only two houses on the estate where the foundling was not discussed at all. One was the residence of Commissioner Fikri Afendi who, when his wife asked him about it at lunch, was satisfied to mutter in a way that Umm Safwat knew only too well and knew meant he wanted the subject closed. When Fikri Afendi wanted a conversation ended, that meant it was over, for he was a man who did not marry a woman who would share his life but one who would serve him. He chose her, because she was pretty and a good cook, and because she knew nothing about the strange world full of sin and evil that lay outside their door.

That was why he was so deeply distressed whenever his wife was invited to call at Mesiha Afendi's house or Afifa and her children came to visit. In his opinion, such visits were unwarranted heresy. A wife was something private that no one else should see, not even the wives of other men. To talk to his wife about the foundling, then, was wicked and unallowable, since it belonged to an immoral and loathsome world ... a world outside their door.

No one even had the courage to bring up the subject in Mesiha Afendi's house. The father was worried — why, no one knew—, and Linda was still in bed with a stomach-ache. It was only that night when Mesiha Afendi and Afifa went to bed, and she fell into a deep sleep, that he stayed awake watching her as she lay there with her long, thin neck round which she frequently wound a scarf and her short, curly black hair her sons had inherited. Mesiha went on watching her for some time, and came close to giving her a poke with his elbow, wanting her to wake up and share his anxiety, but he did not. What troubled him was not something he could talk about openly with anyone, not even his wife Afifa. How could he describe the strange fears that persisted in occurring to him?

His suspicions about Linda's illness had grown to such an extent that he began to think of having the county doctor examine her the next day, not only to see whether she was really sick but also to find out exactly what was wrong. The girl was old enough for marriage, and she was pretty, abundantly healthy, and had plenty of free time. It might be the Devil had led her astray.

Mesiha's heart sank whenever he reached this point in his thoughts; he could actually feel it falling as though it were dropped from a great height. But his fears had no mercy on him: they went on to show him, God forbid, what could happen. The scandal, the disappointment, and the greater bewilderment. Then it would be impossible for the commissioner's son to marry her for a thousand and one reasons. What would he do then, and how could he continue to live on the estate and face everyone?

He was overcome by his thoughts which, obstinate and forcing themselves on him, set his brain on fire and made him toss and turn in bed, as he glared resentfully at the deeply sleeping Afifa, and choked on the tears caught in his throat that did not want to show him mercy, either, by falling.

While he was in the grip of this dreadful nightmare, a question formed itself in his mind: Couldn't he be wrong? What if the foundling were proven, for example, to be a Gharabwa woman's child? Wouldn't he consider these thoughts of his — suspecting his daughter and impugning her honor — a form of madness and idiocy?

Mesiha clung to that thought as though it held the elixir of his salvation. Eagerly he turned it over in his mind, and examined it from all sides. As he did this, his heart began to slow down and resume its normal place in his chest, and breathing freely and easily once more, he yawned as sleep overtook him.

The first thing he did when he got to the office the next morning was ask for the commissioner. When he was told that he was in his office, he knocked on the door with his customary caution and went in. After the exchange of greetings, Fikri Afendi scrutinized him for a long moment, trying to understand the sly purpose behind that morning visit. The chief clerk's visits to his office were few, and behind each one was a motive that was invariably malicious. What mystified Fikri Afendi, however, was that Mesiha did not say much during his stay. He sat and talked a while about the usual things, and then asked in passing what had happened with the foundling. Fikri Afendi answered him in all honesty, but he was astonished when Mesiha began, suddenly and emphatically, to badmouth the Gharabwa, and to insist until he practically swore that the culprit was one of them. Not long afterward, he took his leave with the excuse he had work to do. And Fikri Afendi was left at a loss to explain this sudden prejudice against the migrants.

The commissioner, however, was not allowed much time for puzzlement, since soon there was a knock on his door. In his well-known manner, he bellowed, "Come in!" The caller was Mahboob, the estate mailman. The blue cloth cap was askew on his forehead, his eyes were filled with tears, and he was sobbing convulsively. It was a problem that had brought him, and what a problem it was.

"Mahboob, what's wrong?" asked Fikri Afendi, trying not to laugh.

Mahboob did not reply. He reached a stubby hand into the pouch hanging at his side (its strap had been shortened as much as possible to keep it from dragging on the ground), and took out a letter whose envelope had been carefully opened. He said not one word.

Fikri Afendi took the letter. Turning over the envelope, he found the following written on it in indelible ink:

> To: Abd al-Munim Afendi Awwad
> 34 Gaami Ahmadi Street
> Tanta
> PERSONAL

There was nothing exciting about the address, nor could it be a reason for Mahboob's tearful sobbings. The commissioner would almost have given it back to him had Mahboob not controlled himself, dried his tears, and told him how he first became suspicious of the letter.

Mahboob said that Saadaat, wife of Usta Abdu the truckdriver, who lived on the same farm as Mahboob, had called out to him to stop as he rode his donkey from the big farm to the Delta station. She stopped him at their farm, and asked him to take the letter. When he asked her who wrote it — since it was ridiculous to suppose she had — she said it was from her husband to his relative in Tanta. Mahboob did not debate it with her, since he knew her husband did have a relative in Tanta, and letters from there sometimes came for him. He believed her, and continued on his way to the train. Shortly after he left the farm, however, he began to feel as though that letter — unlike the others he carried — was a thorn pricking his flesh. And accordingly, he found himself reaching a hand into the bag, taking out the letters, and studying that particular one. He looked it over for a few moments, and although he was illiterate, and couldn't tell one person's handwriting from another's, "Something of God's own inspiration told me, 'Mahboob, that's your wife's writing.'" All of a sudden, things he had never thought twice about became clear to him. His wife Zakiya had a relative in Tanta who came to visit them a few weeks ago and stayed three days. This relative of hers was a "gentleman," and Zakiya said he was a student in the Technical College. Despite his looking very mature for a student with his full moustache, beard and overall appearance, Mahboob believed Zakiya and took what she said in good faith. But now — as he held the letter in his hand and felt as though Zakiya's face and scent were in its written characters — there was no more room for good faith. What happened next was that Mahboob changed direction, and instead of going to the station, he went to see Sheikh Ali Abu Ibrahim, the estate's Quran-reciter. Having first carefully opened the envelope and extracted the letter, he asked the sheikh to read it.

Taking the letter, Sheikh Ali got out a pair of glasses with cheap wire frames. After scrutinizing it thoroughly, he read it silently to himself. Scarcely had he finished than he flew at Mahboob.

"May God bring you low! What is this nonsense, boy?"

Mahboob nearly fell from what was already a rather humble height. Now he knew for certain that his suspicions were correct. He turned to Sheikh Ali, kissed his hand, and wet it with his tears, begging him to read the letter out loud. The sheikh obliged, and lo, it was a passionate love letter from his wife Zakiya. And she was not content with that, but wanted to make a fool of him, too, and have him carry the letter to her lover with the other mail, the slut — exploiting him because he didn't know how to read and write.

During the time Mahboob was telling his story, Fikri Afendi nearly died laughing. He couldn't even make an effort to contain his mirth. What was more, as he saw Mahboob becoming more and more agitated, he was seized by an uncontrollable desire to not just laugh, but to snort and guffaw louder than ever before in his life.

When Mahboob had finished, and began to break down again, Fikri Afendi could restrain himself no longer. He erupted in a convulsive fit of laughter, and rang the bell to call in Mesiha Afendi, Ahmad Sultan, and the head overseer who, it happened, was there in the office. Assuming Mahboob's part in the narrative, the commissioner told the story to the others who laughed in his stead. In the meantime, Mahboob went on crying in reckless abandon.

Wiping the tears of laughter from his eyes, Fikri Afendi asked, "Why didn't you go and beat her up, Mahboob?"

"Beat up who, Mr. Commissioner. ... Am I her size?"

With that, Mahboob burst into tears again, and the men around him howled with laughter. They knew Zakiya, tall, heavy, and powerful, and here before them stood Mahboob — short, and skinny, with a voice as weak and slight as an adolescent girl's.

When they had their fill of laughter, the commissioner patted Mahboob on the back, and promised to teach Zakiya a lesson. In fact, he even sent someone to look for her, but then as though in sudden realization, he asked, "Mahboob, do you want a divorce?"

A last tear escaped him, and he said, "Whatever you think's best, sir. I swear by all that's holy that she's a whore, and I bet it was her kid they found this morning. She wants kids, you see, and she thinks it's my fault we don't have any. She's a whore, I tell you."

The commissioner detected a note of indecision in his answer that meant he didn't want a divorce. So, he assured him again that he would devote his whole afternoon to Zakiya, and he'd have her seeing the "noontime stars," before he was through.

*　　　　　*　　　　　*

It would seem it was those same "noontime stars" that were at that moment absorbing Dumyaan. He was carrying the market basket on his way to look for some fish for his brother's household. When he arrived at the stone bridge, however, he came to a halt in the exact middle of the bridge, and stared up at the sun which shone directly overhead. Usually people looking at the sun are unable to withstand its bright light, and they shut their eyes. But Dumyaan had a marvelous ability, the ability to look right at the sun without blinking.

It was not, however, Dumyaan's ability that made some of the peasant children gather to watch him. It was because as he stared up at the sky, he rolled down the left sleeve of his robe, and began to count on it with the fingers of his right hand, saying to himself, "Victorious ... God willing, victorious. ..." Just who was victorious, and how and why it would triumph, Dumyaan did not say, even if anyone had asked him.

The commissioner's house was located right across the canal. Anyone standing at the small balcony window that overlooked the farm had a clear view of everything that took place on the stone bridge and of Dumyaan, too, in that laughable position of his. It was not just anyone who stood there, however; it was a woman, the commissioner's wife Umm Safwat, to be exact. A lady of forty, she was fair-skinned with plump thighs and buttocks. And, in spite of her husband's position, she wore the same kind of fringed kerchief as the "stylish" peasant women, and the same type of loose-fitting, flowered dress. The matter of Dumyaan had been bothering her for some time now. Once she even questioned his sister-in-law Afifa about him, but the chief clerk's wife had evaded giving her an answer. Today, for some reason — maybe it was the huge uproar over the illegitimate baby, the forbidden, and what was right and what wasn't—, she was burning with curiosity. She was a prisoner of her big house, day and night, never visiting nor being visited, except on rare occasions. It was visits that made her life miserable, visits that forced her to flatter the wives of the employees. She would try her best to act sophisticated and refined, but more often than not, her pretense would be discovered, and ashamed and embarrassed, she would go off by herself and cry. And woe to her from Fikri Afendi her husband if she ever made a mistake! After more than twenty years of marriage, she still did not dare to call him anything but "Mr. Fikri," or, at most, in moments of timid confidence, "Abu Safwat."*
There were times when she longed for the days of her early childhood in the house of her peasant father. And sometimes she wished she could do as the peasant women did and bathe in the canal, for example, or bake her own bread and take the perfectly rounded loaves out of the oven the way she had in her father's house.

---

*Among the more traditional Arabs, parents are given an honorific title that is formed by combining either the word *Abu* ("father"), in the man's case, or *Umm* ("mother"), in the woman's, with the name of their eldest son (e.g., Safwat). In the absence of any sons, the parents are called by the name of their eldest daughter — Tr.

Fikri Afendi came from the north, while she was a southerner from the central part of Upper Egypt. Her husband first saw her when he was visiting a relative who ran their train station. He admired her, and in a day and several nights of festivities, he married her.* Ever since, her relations with her family had been nearly severed. Even when her brother came to visit them on the estate — with his scarf, striped *gallabiya*, and elastic-sided boots that were so typical of Upper Egypt —, Fikri Afendi hid the fact that he was visiting. If people asked about the stranger, the commissioner said he was one of the men who worked for his father-in-law and that he came to reassure the old man about his daughter.

Umm Safwat was never able to realize any of the things she longed for. She was obliged to play the role of the haughty, respectable commissioner's wife at all times. There was only one whim she could satisfy without bringing her husband's anger down on her. Dumyaan came often to the house to borrow a cooking pot, a sieve, or a piece of candy, or to bring her messages from Umm Linda. Not once did he come over but she would make him stay and talk. She was in seventh heaven as they chatted, since she could let herself be completely natural. She would ask him to read her fortune in the coffee cup, and that would be but a way of starting a conversation. The strange thing was the way Dumyaan spoke freely to her, talking, for example, about his problems with the chickens, and the troubles he had with his sister-in-law. Sometimes he would cry in front of her like a child, and in spite of herself, she would join him in his tears.

Dumyaan was still standing in the middle of the bridge, and she was still looking down from the balcony window. But her desire to engage in the silly, harmless chatter she enjoyed with Dumyaan was not what kept her awake during that siesta hour. It was rather, the unsolved question that so often made the farm women sleepless: Did Dumyaan have what it took to please a woman? Each time the thought occurred to her, she regarded it as a forbidden, shameful thing — even thinking about it was wrong, she knew. But at that hour — she herself did not know why—, she no longer looked at it the same way. She did not want, God forbid, to sin with anyone, most certainly not Dumyaan. She only wanted to know. Could that be forbidden, too?

The longer she stood at the window with Dumyaan in full view on the bridge, the more she was overwhelmed by her desire to know

---

*The traditional Arab wedding is preceded by seven nights of feasting and dancing — Tr.

until she reached the limits of her self-control.

And so it was that she called for Faatima, one of the many girls who served in the commissioner's house and were counted as laborers working in the field. She called Faatima and asked her to go and bring Dumyaan. She had no clear plan in mind. Nor did she know what she would do if, as usual, he escaped from answering her questions. Should she lead him on gradually, should she trick him, or should she seduce him and go on with it to the end of the game to see if he'd respond? She had no clear plan. But she had determined she would know the truth about Dumyaan, even if it led her to do the impossible.

Dumyaan arrived, laughing and mumbling as usual. The basket hanging from his arm, he was drooling, the spittle all but running from his mouth every time he shook his head or began to laugh. Umm Safwat greeted him warmly, and sat him down on the couch in the bedroom — in spite of his reluctance, for he had an intense aversion to sitting in anyone's presence. This was not the first time Dumyaan had entered the bedroom, since there was nothing suspicious or shameful about his being there. He sat down reluctantly, and she settled herself beside him, and asked him to cast her horoscope for that day. Dumyaan turned his hand over, wet his fingers, and drew with them on the back of his hand, and calculated.

Minutes later, Dumyaan was seen running from the commissioner's house, the basket still on his arm. Some people tried to stop him to ask why he ran, but to no avail.

The fact that Dumyaan had come running out of the commissioner's house did not pass without comment. Since it was something unusual, there must be a secret behind it. And, as long as it had become a secret, it was just as inevitable that tongues would begin to wag.

In general, this was not the only secret that became grist for the gossip-mills. So many of them were uncovered, in fact, that their odor filled the air and began to clog the noses of everyone who lived on the estate. Only a few days had passed since Abd al-Muttalib discovered the foundling, but they were enough to have turned everything on the estate upside down. That baby's mother had to be found, and, as long as her identity was unknown, then, any accusation and any rumor might be the truth. Rumors were rife, and estate tongues went on wagging. Clearly, matters would stay like this until the truth became known.

CHAPTER TWELVE

Matters did not call for Commissioner Fikri Afendi to wait nine months like the Caliph Omar, since in less than ten days he was to discover the criminal. Nor was it by chance that he found her, for much of the credit must go to his own native cunning.

The cotton worm eggs had multiplied in a way that portended danger, despite all Fikri Afendi's efforts. They began by threatening to hatch, and then to overrun, all the land that was planted with cotton. In reality, out of the seven thousand people who lived on the estate, Fikri Afendi was the only one concerned about the worms. The cotton's fate did not interest the peasant farmers one way or the other. Although they planted it, cultivated it, and had to pay for hand-picking it, cleaning it, and even dredging canals around it, cotton was the landowner's crop, nothing more. While it was true the peasant got a third of the crop from the land he farmed, that third dissolved into nothing. It went to cover the costs of the cotton and the other crops, and the loan the peasant took out during the year to buy seed and hire laborers. Even if something was left over after that, it was credited to his account for the coming year. How, then, could the cotton interest him? It was the administration that profited, and it was the administration, in that case, that should take care of it.

The responsibility for this rested squarely on Fikri Afendi's shoulders. Cotton was considered the estate's principal crop, and it did not come cheap. If it were eaten by worms, the *khawaaga* landowner lost thousands of pounds, and Fikri Afendi was ruined, too. As a matter of fact, it was the cotton worm which was the main reason for his losing his last job on an estate, when it hatched in spite of his efforts, and devoured the cotton leaves, destroying the crop. Consequently, Fikri Afendi feared nothing in existence as much as he feared two things: the cotton worm and the landowner. This fear did not crystallize into genuine alarm until the time came to combat the worm while still in the egg. It was a time of terrible testing for Fikri Afendi, his nerves, muscles, future, and all that was in him. Between the chief clerk's malicious joy and intrigues, and the inspector's letters that he wrote himself in his cautious, crafty script, writing and underlining parts in red ink, and between the peasants' indifference, and the dawdling and loafing of the laborers and foremen, Fikri Afendi wore himself to the bone, waking up at the crack of dawn, and not coming back from the field until after the evening call to prayer, invoking the protection of Divine Providence all the while. What he feared most was a lull in the battle, for then the eggs would hatch and calamity ensue. He would lose his job, and live in that hateful degradation to whose misery he preferred death. Like most estate commissioners and managers, Fikri Afendi could not leave an estate if he were fired until he found work somewhere else, since he had no house, no community, and no place to call his own. Accordingly, when an estate commissioner lost his job, he had to plead with the landowner to let his family stay in their house on the estate while he wandered through the area, asking friends and acquaintances, looking for some kind of work, even if only to find a place for his family. ... The worst thing that could happen was for the new employee's family to arrive, with children and furniture, before the former employee found work and a place to stay. ...

That was why Fikri Afendi feared the cotton worm more savagely than death. Likewise, he was desirous of adorning himself with a noble character, because of his conviction that a strong link existed between any sin he might commit and the crawling, black devils that God loosed upon him once a year to test him. He would be severely punished if he had sinned, but if his purity and innocence were proven, the millions upon millions of demons would retreat to their lairs.

Because of his excessive zeal, he would leave before sunrise to scout all the cotton fields, sniffing the air and fearing that, God forbid, his senses would pick up the scent of the worms. The eggs had no smell, but the worms — God save him from the stench which made his heart pound whenever he smelled it ... a strange smell that hung over the field, the cotton, and the early morning ... millions upon millions of small, savage animals devouring every single thing in their path ... like the smell of the grave. ... Fate would decree it so, and one morning early his nose would pick up the scent — like the smell of death as it consumes living things and makes them into long, black worms ... the smell of the living, green leaf as it dies and the creeping, black death feeding off the living green. Fikri Afendi shuddered at the mention, or even the mere thought, of it. And oh, if the *khawaaga* landowner were to catch a whiff of it! Khawaaga Zaghib — nothing on earth unnerved Fikri Afendi more than news of his coming. Even as he gave orders to the stable hands and day laborers to sweep the grounds and to wet down the dust on the road and in front of the mansion, his voice would tremble and betray his agitation.

They said the estate belonged first to one of the princesses, who then sold it to Khawaaga Zaghib, Sr. The present landowner was his eldest son. He was huge and overpowering with thick, yellow hair showing on his chest and arms when he dressed in a shirt, trousers, and white topee to go out on a tour of inspection. He would not smile the entire time, but sat his horse, which no one rode but he, like a massive statue. Fikri Afendi, looking like a wizened monkey on the donkey by his side, spent the whole trip with his eyes fastened on the *khawaaga's* features, while his tongue rattled on in an attempt to make him laugh, and his hand pointed out a newly dredged and deepened canal, or a skillfully made footpath. As the hand gestured and pointed, it also concealed any shortcomings, if any there were, and there always were. Fikri Afendi would pray to God and all the angels and prophets that the *khawaaga's* eyes would not fall upon whatever it was. But they always did, as though created to see only imperfection. The disaster was that he said nothing when he saw it — if he would only say something! But he remained silent, and how unpleasant was his silence at such moments. ...

He was married to a Frenchwoman. On the rare occasions when she came with him to the estate, Fikri Afendi would try to present her with a small basket of the mulberries she loved. Perhaps she would say something in his behalf and cast him in a favorable light, even if it were in that language which he did not understand and which was all she spoke to the *khawaaga*. They said the *khawaaga* had a mistress and no children, and that, if he weren't a Catholic, he would have divorced his wife perhaps and had a son to inherit all this property. They also said, Fikri Afendi being the one who said it, that in his palace overlooking the sea at Sidi Bishr in Alexandria, there was a dining room of pure gold: the chairs were inlaid with the precious metal, and every dish, knife, fork, and spoon was solid gold. They said that Zaghib, Sr., bought it when he invited the king, who was then the sultan, to dinner. They said more than this — they said the Khawaaga, Jr., having fallen on hard times since the death of his father, had in fact sold the estate to the Belgian Land Company and rented it from them, and managed it for the company. That was one story. Another version had it that al-Ahmadi Pasha, the province's millionaire, was thinking of buying it, and was engaged in negotiations with the *khawaaga* and the company. That was hard for everyone to take, because al-Ahmadi Pasha had been a porter in the rice-hulling plant before World War I. He did some trading, made a profit, got rich, and then bought the plant and became a man of influence with buildings and thousands of pounds in the bank. Now he was thinking of buying the princess's estate. The worst part of it all was that they said he was ready to pay the whole thing in cash.

They said many things about the estate and its owner, Khawaaga Zaghib. What mattered, however, was that he was still the landowner, the mere possibility of whose coming caused Fikri Afendi's limbs to tremble, the quiet man whom nothing could induce to break his silence but the sight of a mistake. Then he would not have cared had it been his father who erred, so ruthless was he as he fired men right and left, docked their pay, and sometimes even struck them. And oh, what a heavy hand he had, raised on chicken, pigeon, turkey and wine, when it hit a man and made his ribcage buckle.

The increase in the number of worm eggs, then, was an overwhelming danger that had to be averted. Such an increase meant one thing to Fikri Afendi: the battle was not being fought as it should. That meant the laborers were loafing and the men in charge — overseers, foremen, and supervisors — were playing, not working. While there might be many reasons for that, Fikri Afendi blamed it all on one thing: his donkey's bray. That was what betrayed his coming from far off, and made them act out in front of him the play, "Get Down Lower, Boy, Lower, Girl," that they performed so well. Accordingly, Fikri Afendi eliminated the donkey from his tour of inspection, and began to cover dozens of miles on foot — maybe then he would catch his subordinates in the act of being negligent.

More than once, Fikri Afendi achieved what he wanted, and surprised the rows of laborers from behind. Each time, however, he was somewhat disappointed to find the work in full swing and no evidence of negligence. Once he caught the migrants' boss Arafa sitting in the shade of a sycamore tree playing siga* with the elderly Usta Muhammad, and another time he discovered that Saalih, the overseer, had sent a migrant women to bring his lunch from the farm. Aside from those incidents, however, the work went on as though Arafa did not sit playing siga or Saalih allow himself to short it by the efforts of a laborer!

---

*Siga is a game similar to checkers which is usually played with small stones — Tr.

60

Fikri Afendi, however, did not despair. There had to be negligence somewhere, and it was inevitable that he would find it. The day he came across the shelter that was set up between the stalks of hemp planted around the cotton square, his heart beat fast with the joy of discovery, and he believed he had found it at last. Surely there were laborers resting or loafing beneath that shelter. His efforts, then, were not in vain, and the long, grueling experience of making his inspections on foot without a donkey was not wasted.

Without questioning Arafa or even speaking to him, he hurried toward the shelter as soon as he saw it to catch the laborers sitting in its shade unawares.

The shelter was made from an old gunny sack that was tied at its four corners to four sturdy stalks of hemp. When Fikri Afendi parted the bushes and peered in, he was startled not to find many laborers. As a matter of fact, he found only one. To be precise, it was a female laborer, a woman who lay on her side as though sleeping.

Fikri Afendi's chagrin turned to vicious ill-temper. With his eyes shooting sparks, he snapped at Arafa, "What's this? Why's she sleeping here? Why isn't she out working?"

Smiling in a way that irritated the commissioner even more, Arafa said, "This is Aziza, Mr. Commissioner, sir."

"What Aziza? Aziza who?"

Lowering one corner of his smile and lifting the other, Arafa repeated, "Aziza, Mr. Commissioner. The tale's not fit for your ears."

CHAPTER THIRTEEN

It was as if a rusty bell rang faintly in Fikri Afendi's head. Could she be the sinner he had sought until he abandoned all hope? The very thought was tenuous, but the long line of the boss's smile was even thinner. If he asked him straight out, he'd probably get scared and balk like a donkey that sees a hole in the road. He knew better than anyone else when these people were hiding something they were afraid to have known. He would have to fall back on cunning and patience, and pretend he knew nothing, maybe then he'd succeed in discovering all that lay behind that smiling, tight-lipped mouth.

In the same commissioner's tone he used in the presence of an error, Fikri Afendi demanded, "Is this woman being counted as a laborer?"

The boss, afraid to lie and be punished many times more for that than for his deception, said, "Yes, sir. ... Your servant, sir."

"How can she be counted as a laborer when she's sleeping?"

Humbly, the boss said, "She's a poor, sick woman who can't keep up in the field, Mr. Commissioner, sir."

"Then she shouldn't get paid!" replied Fikri Afendi violently.

Resigning himself to God's will, the boss said, "No, sir. Whatever you think, sir. She won't get paid."

"Oh, really. ..."

With that, the commissioner readied himself for the attack. He didn't mean what would be, but what was: he meant the days that woman had spent resting and not working while her daily pay was falsely credited. The boss knew that, too, and he knew the penalty might be dismissal, or maybe even jail. He did not hold out for long. Of his own accord, he talked. Nor did he come out with it directly, but began with a long introduction about poverty, poor people, and casting bread on the waters. And then he got to the point, and said that Aziza was the mother of the murdered foundling. When the migrants found out, they protected her, because she was a woman, and we all have womenfolk. And when she got sick with the fever, they thought it right she should rest under a shelter in the field so

62

she'd get her pay. She was such an awfully poor woman, and she supported a sick husband and three children.

The commissioner heard him out, his face wearing the same stern expression as before. But near the end of the story, his features began gradually to relax. Then a look of astonishment traced itself on his face, replacing the earlier harshness. The bewildering thing was she was married. If she was married, why would she murder her own child? Fikri Afendi said as much to the boss who replied, "Who knows, sir ... the world's full of troubles."

"What do you mean, 'who knows?'! Have you gone crazy, or has something happened to your brain?! Here's a married woman who kills her baby just like that, and you call it, 'the world's full of troubles'! Is her husband still alive, boy?"

"Yes, sir. ..."

"Does she have any children by him?"

"Yes, sir. ..."

"Did she ever kill her children before this?"

"Never, sir."

"Then, how come she did this time?"

"God knows, sir."

The boss looked as if he never once considered the strangeness of it, or as if, having considered it, he did not regard it as important enough to merit the labor of thought. There was nothing more to the matter than that when the laborers pleaded with him as a favor to let Aziza rest in the shelter during work, he did so willingly, because he knew her, and because he knew her husband and her father. The only thing that worried him was that the commissioner or someone from the administration might find out. That was all that bothered him. And now his biggest concern was how to get around the commissioner so he would overlook this mistake. Accordingly, he resumed his persistent pleadings to forgive them, they were in trouble, sir, and he was the only one who could save them ... and so on down the list of expressions which the boss excelled in pulling out in every predicament.

The commissioner, however, had something else on his mind. Even though he was a little disappointed now that the picture contained no crime, no whore, and no virgin tricked and seduced by a careless young man — even though he was disappointed—, the unsolved puzzle of the woman began to occupy him in a different way. Why would a married woman like that one wrapped in black rags kill her own child?

The boss did not seem to be hiding anything. It could be that no one knew the true story but the Almighty and Aziza.

"Did you ask her why she did it?" said Fikri Afendi to the boss. He replied, "We couldn't get anything out of her. Here she is, sir. You talk to her."

Even without the boss's saying that, Fikri Afendi definitely intended to go over to the shelter and examine this she-wolf. She was lying at the bottom of one of the small canals used to irrigate the squares. Lying on her side, she had drawn her knees up against her stomach, and gripped her head between her elbows, curled up like a fetus in its mother's womb. She didn't look any different from the other women in the migrant army, for clearly she was very dark, or to be precise, her skin was burned dark, seared by the sun's scorching rays that beat down upon her unimpeded all day long. Fikri Afendi, however, did not fail to notice that the inner flesh of her knee was a lighter color, and that her black dress, torn in more than one place, here and there revealed patches of white like circles of sunlight traced on a floor through the chinks in a roof.

Fikri Afendi looked at her a long time, convinced that when she felt his presence over her head she would surely sit up, for example, or straighten herself. But nothing of the kind happened. She went on sleeping without so much as the flicker of an eyelid. It was then that Fikri Afendi spoke to her, "Sit up, girl." As he said it, he prodded her a little with the toe of his shoe.

She neither answered nor sat up, but turned her eyes to face him. Would that she hadn't! Her face was so deeply flushed that the skin was nearly black. In her eyes were flecks of blood, real blood that was only kept from spilling by a thin, glistening curtain. Her teeth were chattering, and although it was barely noticeable, she was shivering all over.

Instinctively, Fikri Afendi laid the back of his hand, which was covered with hair and sweat, on her forehead. He pulled it back at once as though burned, saying, "She's got a fever, boy!"

In answer, the boss said, "She's been like this two days now ... poor woman ... as you can see, sir."

"See what ... she's going to die like this."

The boss found the time had come, and he was quick to add, "Anyway, if you want to cut her pay, sir, really, it's how you see best."

His timing was exactly right, for Fikri Afendi was shaking his head, and saying over and over, "There is no power or strength save in God." That meant at least he agreed to overlook Aziza's resting, and would go on paying her wages.

Fikri Afendi remained standing where he was for a long time like someone who didn't know what to do, looking at the woman curled up in her black rags on the rough ground with its bricks and clods of dirt, turning to stare at the laborers, and then letting his eyes wander over the hateful silence of the brightly lit field. ...

And then suddenly the prone woman screamed — the way a train will sometimes give an unexpected whistle—, and reached out wildly with her hand. Pulling up some hemp stalks by the root, she assailed them with her teeth, biting and gnawing at them, and wailing, "All because of the sweet potato, my dear!"

Alarmed, Fikri Afendi stepped back. After the boss had regained his breath, he told the commissioner, "It's because she talks crazy, sir. Her head's burning up with the fever. ... It's been this way a long time now. ... All day and all night, it's like this ... such things as she says. ... It's plain this woman's seen a lot ... God help her."

CHAPTER FOURTEEN

Even when Aziza was in the best of health, she was no great beauty — she was not even beautiful. Tall and thin, she had a long, thin nose, and she always wore a black square of cloth as a kerchief. Her face was pale, and her eyes, one with a white spot from a long-ago disease, were wide. But she had not always been like that. Once she was a pretty young girl with eyelashes, hair, and breasts, who used kohl on her eyes and clip-clopped in slippers when she went out walking and passed the young men. That was how she was until they married her to Abdallah. Then, too, she had a wedding eve when they dyed her hands and feet with henna, a wedding celebration, a wedding night, presents, and hot water that Abdallah's mother brought her in the *sabaahiya,** a *sabaahiya* that lasted just one day. The very next morning she was in the field.

Her husband had no land to farm; he didn't even have land he could rent. He worked, instead, for a daily wage. He worked one day, and the next ten days he didn't. He depended for his livelihood on seasonal migrant work when he would collect his pay from Hagg Abd al-Rahim, the contractor, and be taken off by the trucks to one of Egypt's many estates in Daqahiliya and Sharqiya provinces, and even Fayyum and Bani Suwaif. But ever since the day he married Aziza, the trucks no longer carried him alone, but began to bring her with him. And instead of the one daily wage, he got two. Aziza and he spent many long years away from their home in other people's villages where they saw much and accumulated little. But they got by. They had children, too: little Abdallah, Naahiya, and Zubaida. They got by, collecting their pay from Hagg Abd al-Rahim during the cotton season and living off that, all of them, the rest of the year. By force and by trickery they got by, sometimes on cheese and

---

*The first day following a couple's wedding night is called the *sabaahiya*. Traditionally, the bride's family prepares and brings them food, and the newlyweds spend the day at leisure, without going to work or performing any domestic chores — Tr.

sometimes on plain bread and salt, but they got by, and that was enough. Until the inevitable happened. Abdallah got sick. It started with abdominal pains on the left side, then they moved to the right, and then they were everywhere. After that, the abdomen itself became swollen. They said to Abdallah, "Cauterize," and he cauterized. Then they told him, "Bilharzia* and splenitis," and the little strength he had left was exhausted as the county hospital's needles were jabbed in his arm, emptying their lacerating poison into his body and making him fall. Sometimes the needles made him dizzy, and they would throw water on him. Every other day he'd have a shot. And every day, to go to the hospital, he had to get up at dawn and be there by seven, or he lost his turn. He would come back in the afternoon or at sunset, holding on to the saddle of one of the villagers' donkeys, supporting himself against it, or walking ten steps, and resting ten.

In spite of all this, Abdallah continued to waste away as though his body were dying by inches, and no power on earth could stop it. Until finally dropsy immobilized him. Actually, it wasn't the sickness that made him sit at home. It was Hagg Abd al-Rahim who defeated him, really, and forced him off the truck. None of his connections or intermediaries were of any use. For, what could the contractor do with him when the estate administration would surely refuse him? Aziza began to cry, and she, too, got down from the truck. "You should go," everyone told her. But she refused and said, "We'll let it pass this year. Maybe we can go together next year." Abdallah became angry and said, "Get going!" And again she refused, saying, "Who could I leave you with?"

And so Aziza stayed at his side. Sometimes she baked bread for the neighbors, and sometimes she gathered animal dung to sell, or walked to the county seat with firewood, and returned with a piaster or two. Once a week or once every ten days, she'd make a day's wages. Abdallah, as he lay in the courtyard of their humble house, his stomach distended, his voice weak, and his pale, gaunt hand caressing little Abdallah on one side and Naahiya and her sister on the other, felt truly sick and disabled, and felt, too, if it weren't for Aziza, they would have all starved to death. Nonetheless, his

---

*Bilharzia (schistosomiasis) is a disease endemic to Egypt. Caused by parasitic flukes, it affects the intestines, liver and spleen. Since the flukes abound in stagnant water and are able to enter the body through the pores of the skin, bilharzia is commonly contracted by peasants who walk barefooted in and around the irrigation canals — Tr.

conscience would not leave him in peace, and he would moan, clench his hands into fists, and stare at the shabby, dilapidated roof with eyes the disease had made larger and wider so they protruded and gleamed strangely, and he would say, "Is this the way it is, God. ... Are you happy my wife has to feed us? ..."

He thought this was all too much for him to bear. Aziza also suffered as she saw him lying there, pale and helpless, his belly swollen. But time — strong, powerful time — soon took everything in hand. Abdallah ceased to feel it was too much for him or Aziza to bear, and she no longer looked at her husband's illness as strange or unnatural. It all became normal. She would go out in the morning, and not return until she had something to bring back. He would guard the house that had nothing in it, watch the children, and bide his time to drink down quantities of the water that Aziza forbade him when she was there, because they had told her his cure lay in keeping it from him.

It became so normal that one day Abdallah, wheedling as an invalid does when illness has made him as temperamental as a child and as demanding as a spoiled little boy, one day Abdallah said to her, "I've got a craving for sweet potato, Aziza."

A sick person's request is sacred, and his family responds as though seeing in it a cure, or a farewell to the world.

"My dear ... with all my heart," said Aziza.

There were no sweet potatoes in the village. There had been a crop planted in Qamarain's *feddan*, but it was long harvested and sold, and the land was now being readied for corn. But Abdallah's request was dear to her heart, and she must try. She knew the villagers, after the sweet potatoes were harvested, had filled the ground full of holes looking for anything the harvester's mattock might have missed, and that no hope remained of finding even the smallest bit of sweet potato. But Abdallah's request was dear to her, and she had to try the impossible. ...

Aziza picked up Abdallah's mattock, which was rusty from lack of use, and headed toward Qamarain's *feddan*. Going straight to the places with the fewest holes, she set to work. She dug down about three feet but found nothing, and moved on to another spot where she put the mattock to work. There, too, she found nothing. She came across just about everything else — old crop roots, potsherds, sand, and some scrap iron—, but she found no sweet potatoes.

And as she was laboring, short of breath, having gathered up the outer skirt of her long, black dress and tied it at her waist the way the men did their *gallabiyas*, it happened that she saw a shadow, then heard a voice, saying, "What are you doing?!"

Even before looking up, she knew it was Muhammad, son of the man who owned the field.

Aziza raised her head and straightened her back, wiped off her sweat, and told him the story, pleading with him to let her go on with the search. Muhammad said many things about holes and how they harmed the soil, covered up the silt, and ruined the crop. But she resumed her pleading and went on begging him until she cried. It would seem that Muhammad became embarrassed. For, he not only agreed to let her go on digging, but said gallantly, "Okay, stand aside."

Stripping off his long, outer robe, he took the mattock from her, and looked around with an experienced eye. Then he picked a spot, and was soon attacking it with the mattock. Aziza sat down not far away, and watched him. She compared the holes she had dug with his and their ways of holding the mattock: in her hands the tool was stronger and heavier than she, but when he held it, there was no doubt he was stronger, he was in control, he was the man, a man who reminded her of Abdallah when her husband was working and his arms and legs would bulge with muscles, and he would breathe hard — not the wheezing gasp of someone who was tired or sick, but the strong, regular panting of a man hard at work.

Muhammad Ibn Qamarain was twenty years old, and everyone was talking about his forthcoming marriage to a relative. He was known to have an evil temper, and did not even hesitate to curse at women. Yet, in his own way he was honest, going straight from the field to his house and back again, unacquainted with the coffeehouses, hashish dens, and other nonsense familiar to the young men and good-for-nothings of the village. Thank God, then, he treated her with kindness; thank God, he did not curse her; and God bless him for volunteering to take up the search for the sweet potatoes!

Muhammad struck the ground with the mattock twice in succession, and then said smiling, laughter in his voice (it may have been the first time she ever saw him smile or heard him laugh), "Take this, ma'am."

And he handed her a small bit of sweet potato that made her as happy as if it were a valuable find. She was on the point of getting up and running to Abdallah with her prize when he told her, "Wait." After aiming a few more blows at the ground with the mattock, he presented her with a sweet potato whose bigness astounded her. For, it wasn't just a little bit of root, but a whole sweet potato about the size of a man's fist or even larger.

Aziza wrapped the potato in the end of her shawl, while her tongue repeated every word, every phrase, every prayer of thanks she knew, and sent them heavenwards, wishing him long life and continued success. Eagerly, joyfully, she turned to make her way back to the village. The sun had almost set, and it was growing late and would be dark by the time she reached home.

But in her eagerness and joy, she failed to see the hole that lay behind her. Accordingly, she was startled to suddenly find she had fallen, half in the hole, and half on the ground.

She was not really sure what happened after that. Things began to happen faster than she was able to understand, or change them. No sooner did she try to get up than Muhammad was at her side in the hole, lending her a hand. All of a sudden, she found herself in his embrace as his arms went around her to lift her up. Although she trembled to find herself in the arms of a strange man, still, that man was only "Frowning Muhammad," who was above suspicion. She began to have doubts, however, when Muhammad did not lift her up or allow her to get up by herself. Scarcely were her suspicions aroused than they became reality — terrified at first, she gathered her strength and shoved him. But even as she struggled, she could see it was useless. Nor could she understand exactly why she had collapsed once she was in his arms. She wanted to resist, but she couldn't; she fought with her last ounce of strength, but without hope. Should she scream so everyone would come running, to be disgraced and have her name dragged through the mud? Should she keep quiet? Bite him? Even her clothes, the only clothing she had, he tore. All she could do was moan, dazed and terrified, until he got up. She cursed him then, but what good did that do? ... He said not a word. For a while he only stood there, looking around. The field was completely empty, and in the distance people and livestock were on their way home. He came toward her. And this time she could have gotten up and run, and hit him with the mattock if she had to, but she didn't. She was still, whimpering like someone who, unjustly oppressed, does not absolve himself of responsibility for his own oppression.

*   *   *

Abdallah was overjoyed by the sweet potato, the children had some, and a bite or two even fell to her share. During the next few days, she was unable to shake off the memory of what happened.

Averting her face, she would damn herself, Ibn Qamarain, the sweet potato, and Abdallah, but she secretly thanked God that no one had seen her, and if Ibn Qamarain were to say anything against her, no one would believe him. After a few days, however, she had forgotten the incident entirely. Nothing erases a person's memory so much as the persistent search for something to eat. People who do not forget are people who have time to remember and to go on remembering. Aziza began the day like a madwoman, running here and there to find bread for that day. She came back completely exhausted, no sooner laying her head on the straw pillow than she was overwhelmed by fatigue, far more potent than any sleep, a long stupor from which she was awakened by that secret voice which woke her each dawn, a voice speaking to her of food, the empty house, and her family's hungry, open mouths.

Even when she stopped having her period, she did not pay much attention. Her cycle was often irregular: she'd stop menstruating, become regular again, and then she'd go for months without having a period. She did not realize what had happened until she began to feel pregnant. Even then and in spite of all the signs, she didn't really believe it. It had only happened once, no, twice — could this be? — and all because of a sweet potato?!

The most terrible thing was Abdallah. He had not come near her since their daughter Zubaida was born. Everyone knew that. What would he say, and what would everyone else say? He would never kill her, he wouldn't be able to. No one else would, either, no one could. But it would be easier for her to be killed than to have Abdallah and everyone know.

There was no way out, then, but to get rid of this menacing evil that lay somewhere in her belly, growing bigger every day, filling her, and not resting until it destroyed her. Aziza tried everything. Stalks of jew's mallow, turning the handmill on her stomach, and jumping from the roof — she tried them all. But it was a bastard, in more senses than one, and nothing she did had any effect. Instead, it went on getting bigger every day — it even began to kick—, and the only thing between it and her being disgraced was a thick, strong belt that she wore in hatred and might as though wanting to choke it to death in her belly before it killed her.

The belt did much to hide her stomach. She also let the bosom of her wide, black robe hang down loosely over an outer belt, and when she walked, stood, slept, or talked, she was careful to always do so in a way that left no room for suspicion. This caused her great pain, and she suffered terrible agony of mind and spirit without even the right to complain — and sometimes complaining can help take away our pain. She endured, and kept silent. At night her condition would threaten to overwhelm her, and she would go up to the roof like a thief, loosen her belts, and sit as she liked. Able at last to breathe freely, she would lift her hands, her eyes, and her spirit to the heavens, and beseech God to save her — if not for her sake, then for the sake of the prostrate, disabled Abdallah.

Every night and every minute she prayed, but none of her prayers was answered. What happened instead was something even more bitter: the cotton season arrived, and the town crier proclaimed throughout the village ... "Seven piasters for everybody! Pay days twice a month! Pass the word!"

She had to go this year, or they would perish. When she stayed at home last year, they saw starvation with their own eyes, and lived on empty bellies. She must go. Abdallah told her so, and everyone else did, too. This time she said, "You don't have to tell me, I'm going."

She got her supplies and pressed Abdallah's hand tightly as she said good-bye. Then she kissed little Abdallah, embraced him, and cried. They all cried, and insisted on going with her just as far as "the machine."

The truck filled with people, the driver honked the horn, and the heavy vehicle pulled out. As it began to move, the laborers' voices burst forth, singing of loved ones and exile, and blaming fate. Strangely enough, after the first sobs had ceased to rattle in Aziza's throat and she grew quiet, she started to sing along. Gradually, she began to feel she was leaving the land of poverty, sickness, and sweet potatoes behind, and entering a secure, new life.

In the flood of work that followed, Aziza forgot everything — herself, Abdallah, and the village. But there were times when she remembered her belly and what it held, and the belts around it. There were other times when she forgot. Forgetting and remembering were but a small part of the many things that beat upon her in successive waves: the sun, rising as her back was bent over the cotton plants, and setting as she pushed a dry morsel into her mouth; the day with its summer heat, sweat, and thin bamboo switches whose blows were felt clear to the bone; and the night with its stupor, weary lassitude, and never-to-be-explained dreams.

One day, however, after the midday rest, she was forced to remember everything. Something flashed through her mind the way a treacherous blade gleams before becoming lodged in its victim's body. She felt the beginnings of the cursed labor pains dig into her backbone and then coil around her belly, squeezing her. She felt the damnable evil she carried rap on the wall of her stomach and demand to be let out. It pounded in persistence and determination, continuously, each blow louder and more painful than the last, as though it was going to knock down the wall.

None of her fellow-villagers among the migrant workers knew of her secret. How could they know when they only saw each other bending over the cotton, or strewn about in worn-out, sleeping piles, on their way to the field with eyes still closed by sleep, or coming home, blinded by tiredness and the dust of the field? They had enough to do to worry about themselves, everyone had his own troubles, and no one had even the chance to say "ouch" when something hurt.

But tomorrow they would know. That wasn't the worst of it. The worst would come when she went back with them to the village and to Abdallah, when she went back as the mother of a child who wasn't his. Wouldn't death be easier?

The pains started coming closer together. Scarcely did the boss blow on his whistle and the day end than her face was as pale as death. Even then the woman working next to her did not notice. Aziza, silent, resolute, bore it without a murmur. She left the field, washed like the others, and walked along the path as they did, pausing for a moment when the pains came, then hurrying on once they subsided. When it was suppertime, she ate with the rest, even though the only thing she wanted was a chance to undo the belt constricting her stomach. Terrified, she felt the pain of her belly's contracting within that belt, pain such as no one could endure, not human being, nor rock, nor jinn. She herself did not know by what inhuman power she bore it, without giving the least sign of what she was going through. And all because of a sweet potato, no, all because of one moment in which she did not resist. That moment, which accompanied her for seven months, was pursuing her like a permanent curse. Why did she let him have his way with her? She told herself she hadn't consented, but a voice within her replied, "But you didn't refuse, God damn you." Hopelessly, she heard the voice say, "You knew it was shameful, forbidden. You didn't fight him the way you should have. You didn't scream, and you said, 'The scandal.' Well, here you are with a bigger scandal. Let yourself be dragged through the mud, then, Aziza. Get your fill of scandal, because if you hadn't given in for a moment, it wouldn't have happened." A moment. One moment of weakness from her, she who fought her own nature when Abdallah lay down and did not get up, she who withstood the nights when she wanted him and couldn't have him. ... Could that be why she had weakened in that moment, the moment she was taken by Muhammad Ibn Qamarain. ...

*   *   *

She had to wait until the migrant workers went to sleep, and then get as far away from them as she could to give birth. Childbirth, however, is not a matter of willpower. Her stomach was soon swept by continuous storms, and it was not long before her water broke. Her neighbors were lying down in bed, and her neighbors' neighbors and most of the migrants were still awake. The woman who slept next to her asked her what was wrong, and her clothing soaked through and her stomach on fire, she said, "It's my head."

There was no escaping the inevitable. If she didn't hurry, she would give birth right where she was within sight and hearing of all the migrant workers.

She rose, half-crouching. No one paid her any attention, since everyone supposed she was going to relieve herself. No sooner had she moved a few yards away from them and been swallowed up a little in the darkness than she doubled up with pain. Nonetheless, she did not forget the egg she had borrowed or the half-burned piece of dry willow stick. She clutched one of them in either hand.

She kept on until she reached the bank of the big canal, and then continued along it until she could walk no further. All that, and she was not yet very far from the migrant workers. They were still within earshot, their voices reached her, and had it not been for the darkness that lay between them, they would have seen her and known what she was about to do.

Putting the dry willow stick between her teeth, she squatted on the ground. As each successive wave of pain surged within her, she sank her teeth to their roots in the dry wood, and squeezed a handful of moist earth from the canal until, its moisture gone, it became hard, and she flung it aside.

Nor did she forget what she must do. As soon as the baby's head appeared, she broke the egg, and smeared herself with its slippery contents in the hope of helping the head to slide out.

And finally the baby came. ...

It slipped out all at once, and as though her soul flowed out with it, she grew a little dizzy, and then lost consciousness for a moment. It was only for a short moment, but when she came to herself, she heard, she truly heard, a soft cooing sound. It was the baby, without a doubt. Then, all of a sudden, it gave a cry. A cry that seemed to her as if it filled the whole world, and could be heard by everyone.

She had not prepared herself for that moment. She had thought

74

only about ridding herself of the evil swelling that had exhausted her for so long. Let her abandon it afterwards, or let whatever happened, happen. Now that she had freed herself from it, it was crying, and threatening her with a bigger scandal than ever. Only seven months in the womb, it was yet alive and screaming. She reached out a trembling, unsteady hand, and fumbled with the living, human mass until, finding its mouth, she stuck in her little finger despite herself. ... It was the real mouth of a suckling infant, toothless, a mouth that no sooner felt her finger than it began to make certain movements, and suck on it. The child suckled her finger for a moment. A brief moment, but it electrified her. A strange, violent feeling flowed from that small, fleshy cave to her finger, her arm, and then her whole body. Like a lightning flash, she realized that — despite everything and despite what she had suffered — this baby was her child, and she was its mother. And her hand left its mouth, and groping in the darkness, tried to draw the child nearer.

She was not the actor in this, since she did it without thinking. In reality, she did not think at all. It was as though her arm moved and pulled the baby to her of its own volition.

But all this took no more than a moment. Afterwards the child cried. Her hand went swiftly back to close its mouth. The small opening tried to free itself from the fingers laid across it, and their pressure increased. She was afraid the baby would start crying again if she lifted her hand, and she kept it there by force.

All at once, Aziza came to herself, and found her hand pressed tightly over the baby's mouth. At the same moment, she sensed that the child was still, too still. And in a hoarse, frightened, trembling voice, she cried, "Oh, my God!"

She stayed where she was for a little while. Rigid, unable to move, she did not stir until finally, trembling and afraid, her only thought to get away, she began to crawl on her belly toward the bed of rice straw on which she slept.

Her neighbors and the other migrant workers were asleep. The slab of red rock on which she laid her head witnessed no tears, and Umm al-Hasan, the woman who slept beside her, heard no moans. Nor did Aziza sleep, for all night long she felt as though the Delta train were pushing her toward a collision with the station, crushing her between its iron frame and the iron force of the impact.

Before sunrise, with amazing strength, she was hard at work in the cotton row with the laborers, her back bent, and her eyes searching distractedly for cotton worm eggs.

*   *   *

75

Everything went exactly as she wanted. Even when the commissioner came, and she broke into a cold sweat, her heart pounding, she controlled herself mightily, and passed before him, and he did not stop her as she went by. And when the police came, no one suspected her. She was not even called to appear before the prosecuting attorney. The only thing that happened was that, as she was coming back from the field with the laborers before sunset, it occurred to her to take a different route, and instead of going to the migrant camp by way of the canal, to take the path that passed by the big canal. She did not know why. She actually began to walk in that direction, but shivering suddenly, she hurriedly turned back.

She ate supper with the laborers, and strangely enough, she found her appetite was better than usual. When she went to her straw bed and stone pillow, nothing concerned her but the joy of her release. It was as if that emotion had taken over, anaesthetizing her body, and suppressing all her pain.

At dawn she woke up with the other laborers. With the first rays of the sun, it seemed to her that worry was forever behind her, and she was as free as a bird, having saved herself without anyone's rejoicing at her misfortune, or condemning her for the evil swelling that had brought her so close to death. The morning appeared very beautiful in her eyes, and it seemed as though everything would go just as she wanted, and as though God was with her.

And on her way to the field, she came out of her hateful, self-imposed isolation for the first time. She was intoxicated with the feeling that there was no longer anything to keep her from being like everyone else. She was free to mix with people, as they were with her, she was able to talk with them, and they could laugh with her. ...

The tense line of her face relaxed, and perhaps for the first time in months, she washed and combed her hair. She looked unusually gay and cheerful, and she even joined in with the laborers as they sang a wedding song during work, the bride and groom serenading one another, and the laborers escorting them in solemn procession as they sang in unison.

*   *   *

But everything did not go exactly as Aziza wanted.

Two days later she began to run a fever, and she felt a continuous throbbing in her joints.

On the third day the fever became fires that rose in waves of heat from her skin and abdomen.

She had developed puerperal fever.

But she didn't know what she had, nor did she see any connection between giving birth in the open air by the canal bank, and what was happening to her now. The only thing she knew was that her body had begun to betray her, no longer obeying her awake or asleep, and she was unable to keep up in the field.

But all the pain and fever in the world could not keep her from working, and she continued to go out and come back, and work her row like the others. She would grow dizzy, everything would swim before her eyes, and she would feel hazy and confused, but she drove herself on by force of will, fought her weakness, bent over the cotton, and worked.

She did not exactly know what happened on the fourth or fifth day. She was in the line of laborers, and they asked her, "Aziza, what's wrong?" and she did not answer. Suddenly she fell where she stood. When she came to, she found herself beneath the shelter. But scarcely had she regained consciousness than she began to scream as though they betrayed her and prevented her from working. She actually stood up, wanting to go on with her work, but she grew dizzy, her legs trembled under her, and she fell. When she awoke, she found herself wet with the water they had thrown on her.

Despite a sore throat, constant chills, and fever buzzing in her body, she was still happy that her plan was succeeding, and that no one knew — or would ever know — that she was the criminal.

*   *   ,   *

But her plan was destined to fail for a reason she did not take into account.

Her fever grew worse. ...

And Aziza became delirious, and began to talk.

Umm al-Hasan, who slept near her, started hearing incoherent ramblings about the sweet potato, Ibn Qamarain, Abdallah, and the baby that wouldn't stop crying.

And from her scattered words, the whispers of the women, and what they added, the story was pieced together and became news.

Soon it was traveling from neighbor to neighbor. It crept around their big straw baskets, leaped over the cooking fires, and rummaged in the straw where they slept, pausing at every listening ear.

Not a single ear did the news pass without stopping. And not one ear let it go by without stopping it in turn, examining it, and hesitating a long time whether to believe it. Had the walls had ears, they, too, would have heard it.

Nonetheless, the news never crossed the open area behind the stables. The laborers were as intent on concealing it as though it were their own secret, or some kind of deformity that must be kept away from other people's eyes, ears, and tongues. Even among themselves they said little. The men were content to chew their lips, Aziza and her plight having stopped them from making any other comment. The women put the story aside, and Aziza became their only concern. They fed her, made her drink, helped her to and from the field, worked her row for her, and did not allow her to do anything but bend over and pretend to be working when the commissioner or the overseers went by.

When the news reached Arafa, the migrants' boss, he consulted the older men, and they decided Aziza should stop working entirely, and rest.

Aziza would not agree to that at all until they told her nothing would happen to her wages, and her daily pay would continue. Her greatest fear was that, if she stopped, her wages would end, too, and Abdallah and her children would starve.

When Aziza stopped working and agreed to rest, her heart reassured that her wages would be paid, it was as though the sickness had amassed all its power for that moment. Aziza felt, as if suddenly, that she was truly sick, and that the sickness had overpowered her until she could no longer move.

CHAPTER FIFTEEN

Although the commissioner was the first to hear Aziza's story, the news reached the big farm before him. That was because it was news the people of the estate had waited a long time to hear, and they snatched it up with great eagerness. For, not only did it hold a solution to the mystery that had baffled them, but it was a satisfactory solution, as well. It was exactly the answer they wanted, and had feared would be otherwise. It soothed their hearts, set their minds at rest, and restored their confidence in themselves, their morals, their women, and their worth, that confidence which had faltered and been shaken, which had been ringed around by doubts, and made the object of insolent gossip ever since Abd al-Muttalib first came upon the foundling.

From the jubilation with which the news was received on the farm, you would have imagined that, had there been no Aziza and no sweet potato, everyone would have taken it upon himself to create his own Aziza, and assigned to her all kinds of sweet potatoes, corncobs, or what-have-you, and his tale would have made the rounds, spread like wildfire, and in the end, become the truth. People must regain their faith, and if they can't recover it in the form of truth, then let it be as half-truth. Faith will swear to it, and make it truth. People want to believe in something, no matter what shape their belief may take. And if they can't find something in real life to believe, they will believe in stories.

The big farm rejoiced at the news, along with its peasants, *ustas*, and employees — even the passersby on its roads were overjoyed. Every time one farm resident met another, he shouted, "Didn't I tell you. ... Damned if I didn't say it was those migrants from the very start. Now do you believe it? ..."

The other would confirm that he had, and he did, all but swearing to it himself, and their conversation would turn from the foundling to the migrant workers in their status as the responsible party.

That was what happened. Scarcely were the residents of the farm reassured that they themselves were off the hook than their thoughts began to turn to the Gharabwa whose very existence they had ignored until that moment, hardly aware that they were living on estate land. But as the news about Aziza and her bastard spread, the migrants became more and more the focus of all attention and interest — but what sort of interest?

The news did not affect the important peasants and farmers, except to stir up their latent aversion and disgust for the Gharabwa. Any mention of the migrants was now preceded or followed by a string of insults and a flood of spittle ... as though, in their opinion, the migrants were a kind of human scum that descended on their estate once or twice a year like an unavoidable plague. How do you think they felt when they discovered that something forbidden like the thing that happened a few days ago came from that scum, and that it tried to hide everything, and blame it on *them*? The migrant workers themselves became, for all intents and purposes, forbidden, as though all members of the human race were legitimate, respectable creatures but they. How loathsome did the forbidden become when it committed what was forbidden!

The peasant women were of the same opinion as their husbands and fathers. Stranger yet, they were more fanatical and prejudiced than the men as though begrudging that a migrant woman could become pregnant and bear a child the way they did, even if it were only illicitly.

*   *   *

Mesiha Afendi came home that day in unusually high spirits. His happiness even brought him to the point of recklessness, for he promised his wife she could slaughter several chickens for them to feast on that very day.

Dumyaan whooped with joy at the idea, not because he would eat the heads and wings as he always did when they slaughtered chickens, but because it meant he would be allowed to pluck the feathers, and more important, cut open the gizzards. His greatest joy was to remove the insides of a chicken or a duck, take out the gizzard and run a knife along it, slicing it in half, and feel the yellow stones he found inside, then to remove the inner skin that came off all at once in your hand, without tearing and without your making the least effort. Afterwards, the gizzard would be so clean Dumyaan could almost gobble it down raw. His happiness, however, stemmed not only from his role in cleaning the birds, but also because there would be meat on the table, and because he had a secret longing deep in his heart that never lost its allure: to one day open up a gizzard, and find the diamond treasure he once heard about from his grandmother.

Linda laughed at her father's teasing, for it was seldom that he joked with her. Finding the opportunity suitable, she asked him to let her visit Umm Ibrahim, since the poor woman was sick and had sent for her. Linda did not go out as a rule, except to visit the commissioner's family, or if she were invited, to attend the weddings of the more important peasant families. But Mesiha Afendi was in such a good mood he would have allowed almost anything, even something unprecedented. He threw a sidelong glance at Umm Linda as though to ask her advice, and she raised her eyebrows so high it seemed her thin neck had stretched, too, and grown even longer, saying, "It's up to you."

In jovial tones, Mesiha Afendi said, "All right ... you can go, Miss Linda. But be careful you don't catch anything, you know those peasants' houses are full of germs."

*   *   *

Commissioner Fikri Afendi deserved to be the happiest individual on the estate, for he was the one who, with a combination of intelligence and instinct, had pointed to the migrant workers from the very first, and declared they were the culprits. Moreover, he was the one who had tirelessly persisted until his efforts were crowned with success, his knowledge of human nature was confirmed, and the criminal was found among the migrant workers.

But there were no signs of joy and no glad tidings of victory on his face when he returned to the farm. On the contrary, his expression was clouded, and contained disappointment and indications of thoughtfulness. ... Even when he met Mahboob the mailman who was living again with Zakiya, the commissioner having undertaken to return her to her senses, and to reconcile the couple (even making her kiss Mahboob's feet in his presence, while Mahboob called for help and refused, saying she'd take it out on him once she got him home alone), yes, even when he met Mahboob, the mailbag still hanging at his side, for even though the mailman's working day was over when the four o'clock train went by, he never liked to have people see him without it under his arm as though wanting to set himself apart from everyone, when he met Mahboob who saw him looking troubled, the mailman wanted, as usual, to cheer him up. Accordingly, he told him that ever since he found his wife out, he had been learning to read and write from Sheikh Abu Ibrahim so Zakiya would be unable to take advantage of him again. The commissioner

81

did not laugh. He did not even answer Mahboob, nor did he pay him the least attention. As soon as he dismounted from his donkey, he headed at once for home where he told his wife he wanted coffee. When she brought it she found him asleep in a chair, and did not want to wake him.

As he dozed, Fikri Afendi saw himself sleeping with Aziza beneath the shelter, watched by all the laborers. Her husband, his belly swollen, stood working the cotton row with the others. He watched them, too, but only said, "Ain't you ashamed, Mr. Commissioner, sir. ... You shouldn't do that. ... She's sick."

Fikri Afendi awoke, feeling suffocated, as though suffering from a nightmare.

*   *   *

A heavy rain of curses and abuse directed at the migrant workers continued all day long, even from Junaidi who owned the store, and was the sole person who profited from their presence on the estate. He damned them even to their faces, and showed his aversion to their many outstetched hands by telling them it disgusted him to even touch their *niklas* and *mallims* as though the coins, too, were bastards that came from sin, and were going to sin, and touching them was forbidden.

The only people on the estate with a different opinion that evening were the peasants' children. During the daytime they did as everyone else, and each time they met a migrant woman, they would start drumming on an old piece of tin, and parade behind her. But when night came they saw things differently. Like all children, the estate children loved the nighttime and the chance to play after dark. Night, when the open land that surrounded the farm was filled with moonlight, nighttime rustlings, the croaking of frogs, and the smell with which darkness wrapped the earth, for even the green crops gave forth a special smell at night as though reserving their most fragrant scents for then. At that time the boys would forget about the day's quarrels, grudges, and petty spites. They would even forget about their fathers and their scoldings, and the difficult day to come. It was as though they remembered nothing but being children of their moment, sons of the night and the earth, brothers of the frogs and the stars, and lovers of that clean, tender moon. They played hide-and-seek, cops and robbers, and many other games.* They would start off with one, and abandon it after two rounds to move,

---

*The other two children's games mentioned in the text are *darabuna*

lightly and easily, to another and then another, laughing uproariously without anything to disturb their happiness.

That night one of the boys suggested they go and watch the migrant workers and their children. The boy who came up with the idea was himself astounded at the tremendous roar of approval that greeted his proposal, since he had been half-afraid to suggest it. There was an understanding among the peasants that their children should not play with the migrant workers' children, nor should they even go near them, as though they would catch leprosy if they did. No one asked why there was such a ban, or tried to dispute it. There are many things that are forbidden to children which they are unable to discuss. Can anyone argue with his father when he tells him, "This is wrong," or "That is forbidden"? When words such as these are used, a boy must do as he is told, and he doesn't ask how much one-third of three is.

The boys cheered their friend's suggestion even though they all knew it was wrong, a disgraceful thing to do. When they found they were all agreed, their high spirits and enthusiasm for carrying out the suggestion increased, as if it were no longer forbidden, as though the forbidden had clearly become permissable, and as though the forbidden were no longer forbidden if everyone agreed to it.

Almost immediately they began to race each other to see who could reach the migrant camp first as though a miracle awaited them there, or as though, at the very least, they would see the woman they had heard their fathers and mothers describe with the ugliest words, and accuse of the most horrible things.

But no sooner did the racing boys cross the stone bridge that separated the big farm from the administration buildings, mansion, storehouses, threshing floor and stables, and arrive at what lay behind the latter, seeing in the darkness the baskets and clay jars piled up and scattered like signposts specially erected to mark the

---

muna lamma 'ammuna ("They hit us so much we couldn't see"), muna being a nonsense word; and al-hagar daqdaq(a) wa sarah(a) ("Who has the rock?"). The first of these games is played by two groups of children. One team runs away and hides, while the other goes out to look for them, leaving a child behind to guard their base. The first team then tries to steal back and hit the guard without being caught by the others. If one of them is caught, the two teams exchange places. In the second game, a group of children secretly pass around a rock while squatting on the ground in a circle. Another child, who sits in the middle of the circle, tries to guess which of them has the rock. If he is correct, that child takes his place in the middle. (From a personal interview with Dr. Idris, September, 1977.) — Tr.

migrants' camp, no sooner did they see all this than they stopped running. Then, one by one, they began to tiptoe to the place where the migrant children played, which must be the threshing-floor yard. They were very much afraid as they crept through the migrant camp, as though passing near a tribe of jinn that had stopped there to sleep. But despite their great fear, they couldn't keep from laughing. They heard the sounds of snoring rising from the migrants, which not being entirely even, sounded like the croaking of the frogs in the rice field and nearby canal. The boys laughed, because the frogs were croaking, too, and it seemed as though the migrant workers were snoring in reply, and each time the migrants snored, the frogs croaked back an answer.

The migrant children were indeed playing in the threshing-floor yard. It was far from their tired, sleeping parents, and at the same time, it was removed from the place where the farm children played. No one forbade them to go near the estate children, but from the way the peasants treated them they understood it was taboo, and it was their duty to stay as far away as possible from the farm and its children.

The farm boys stood some distance away and watched. For a while they stayed where they were as though expecting some kind of scolding or protest, but when none came, they moved closer. The threshing floor was big and roomy, and there were enormous heaps of straw from the threshing machine that were nearly as high as the mansion itself. There were also huge piles of wheat, and threshing sleds brought in by peasants who refused to machine-thresh their wheat, preferring to do it by sled even if that took days longer. Wheat threshed by sled, they would say, had a higher yield, while the machine consumed at least a third of the crop with its sinister, excessive speed. For playing, the migrant children had picked a roomy, uncrowded spot that was surrounded on all sides by piles of wheat and straw. Behind and inside the piles the farm children crowded to watch. For a long time they understood nothing of what went on before them as if seeing children who belonged to another race or religion. The migrant children's language was unintelligible, their games were strange, and even their laughter seemed completely different from human beings'.

After a while, however, they began to understand something of what went on. It seemed the migrant children were acting out a play. One of them had put something like a bread basket on top of his head to act out the role of a female cheese-seller, another played the part of a policeman, and a musical dialogue was taking place between the two. The policeman was belligerent and demanded money, while the cheese-seller flounced around, and tried to bribe him with a piece of cheese as "she" enumerated its virtues. The sergeant refused, wanting money, and reprimanded "her" courteously. Well, these children certainly had a strange way of talking, and an equally strange way of playing. If they hadn't known the Gharabwa word for "cheese," they wouldn't have understood a thing. The Gharabwa, then, had their games, too, games which they didn't know. Why then did their fathers and everyone on the farm despise them so much? If only they would agree to let them play, too. ...

This was only a thought that occurred to the farm boys, but it was as if they all thought it at the same time. As usual, the idea immediately moved from their brains to their tongues, and then to their bodies and legs. Leaving their hiding places, they came out toward the migrant children. It took no more than a few words: Will you play with us? We will! At once a great cheer rose up from the two groups of children, a cheer that brought the guard Abd al-Muttalib from the canal, and made him chase after them in hot pursuit until he drove them away from the threshing floor. But the farm children had cunningly proposed to the others that they all go and play behind the irrigation machine where there was plenty of room far away from Abd al-Muttalib, the farm, and the migrant camp.

As they played, children mixed with children. The farm boys discovered the other boys' faces were all different from one another's, and they did not all look alike as they had thought before. And their expressions were kind and good-natured. They could laugh, too, and every boy had a name. Soon they even learned some of them: Misbaah, Badawi, Hasan, and the dark boy was Sinjar. They had a comedian, too, a boy as thin as a stalk of jew's mallow, but he made you die laughing.

That night the children returned unwillingly to their homes on the farm, for they had great fun playing with the migrant workers' children. They learned new games from them, too. There was the game of ten-and-twenty, for example, where one boy laid his skullcap on a dirt pile, and they measured off ten paces from the pile, and twenty from another direction. The two boys who were racing stood one at each point, and if the one who was ten paces away could run to the pile, pick up the cap, and get back to his place before his comrade, who was twenty paces away, caught him, he was the winner.

Silently, stealthily, the boys returned to their beds, their minds made up to go and play every night with the Gharabwa children. They also resolved to hide their plan from their parents even if Abd al-Muttalib informed on them.

CHAPTER SIXTEEN

By the light of a five-candlepower lamp, its glass carefully cleaned to let through as much illumination as possible, which was set on a wooden shelf high on the wall, the room looked unusually tidy and well kept for the home of a peasant. The four-poster bed, so high you almost needed a ladder to climb into it, was spotless and carefully made. The bed skirt hid the jumble of items and foodstuffs that were stored underneath, and the border of cloth above adorned the mosquito netting. Facing the bed stood a wardrobe: a crack in its mirror was disguised by a drawing in white lead of a tree with flowers and fruit. Next to the bed sat a couch with armrests, covered with a white cloth that had been washed with too much bluing. Although the bare, earthen floor was laid with neither wood nor tile, it was swept clean, sprinkled with water to reduce the dust, and overlaid with a fine layer of sand. The water jugs stood in the window, wearing their metal stoppers, and a piece of muslin covered them as an added measure of cleanliness and gentility. In short, everything in the room tried to look its very best.

Only two people were present in the room: Umm Ibrahim who lay on the bed in perfect, glowing health (though anyone hearing her moan would have thought she must be dying), and Linda who sat in the room's only chair, overwhelmed by the strange house she had entered for the first time. With a woman's eye for detail, she studied everything, and marvelled — she who so rarely left their own house and rooms that just to visit someone else's home, even that of Sheikh Abu Ibrahim, the Quran-reciter, was a novelty that left her breathless.

It was Umm Ibrahim who took on the greater burden of what little conversation there was. She did not chatter as easily and incessantly as usual, however; her conversation was erratic and full of pauses as if she was preoccupied, or expected something to happen. Linda listened most of the time, joining in the conversation once in a while, and responding with a sentence or a short, nervous laugh as if she was afraid of something, or wanted to be. Really, she was in splendid looks. Her face was bright and rosy (having been lightly dusted with a barely visible coat of powder), and her hair was glossy and styled so one lock fell loosely on her forehead. Her nose, her features, her expression, and everything about her were all so elegant and beautiful they could hardly be compared to the humble room in which she sat, especially since she wore the newest and best of her three dresses, the one she had made on her last visit to her relatives in Cairo's Shubra. ...

Umm Ibrahim had made colossal efforts during the few days following her promise to Ahmad Afendi Sultan at the mosque. The obstacles before her were enormous, and not easily surmountable. It was hard enough to even be alone with Linda, so what were the chances of having a long conversation with her? And a long conversation was a must. Although Linda was more than old enough for marriage, she was still green as grass. Then, too, she was smart and educated. For all Umm Ibrahim's experience, she was an ignorant woman who had never been off the estate. It was very dangerous, then, for her to talk to Linda, especially about such delicate and shocking matters.

But Umm Ibrahim was able to overcome the obstacles. For, contrary to her expectations, Linda responded to what she had to say in a way she never imagined. Umm Ibrahim had used an approach that never failed: men and their secrets. Men, that closed world totally removed from Linda and everything she heard, those rough beings who seemed so much more powerful and fierce than her father and young brothers, and who, when she saw them, made her shy nervously in spite of herself, and nearly run away. Umm Ibrahim began to tell her about men and what made them tick in the manner of a worldly, experienced woman. She talked about the physical aspect that men never spoke of with women but only among themselves, and that women discussed only in confidential whispers, the kind of talk that never failed to start a conversation and loosen the shyest tongue.

Linda responded, and listened attentively from the very first word, though she was wary of taking part in the conversation herself. But after a while she began to feign ignorance, and now and then ask questions, maybe to be sure of the information, and maybe to hear the words said once again. Then she started making quick, embarrassed comments, while Umm Ibrahim watched her with the shrewdness of a skillful fisherman who patiently waits for the fish to swallow the bait, and then begins, slowly and gently, to pull in the line, without frightening his catch away. So did Umm Ibrahim switch the conversation from generalities about men to specifics. She talked about the different kinds of men, and classified them, putting the strong men in one category, the virile in another, and the weak, good-for-nothings in a third. It was very natural that she would start to integrate generalities and particulars, and to use some of the well-known men on the estate as examples. That was how the name of Ahmad Sultan came up. Umm Ibrahim took a long time to list what was known about him, and she gave him as the most forceful example of manhood, strength, and virility. Here Linda became embarrassed, and all but stopped listening, but it was inevitable that Umm Ibrahim's persistence would overcome her shyness, and open her virginal ears. It was the persistence of an expert, teasing and titillating, the persistence of a woman who knew how to speak and then fall silent just when her listener's curiosity had reached its peak, and who knew how to break off the conversation at once if she saw real fear that would be followed by rejection, infiltrate her listener because of terror at what she said, leaving it to the days and the hours, solitary reflection, and careful scrutiny of the new, forbidden thing to have an effect, cause the iron to yield, and make the rejected acceptable, reasonable, and desirable.

So it was that Linda began to believe a number of things. She believed it was possible for a girl to enjoy a woman's pleasures without sacrificing her virginity, and she came to accept that she herself was miserable and deprived of life's greatest joy, and would remain that way until she got married, and God only knew when that would happen. She became convinced that a woman's body needed something, and that something was a man. And Umm Ibrahim made sure that when Linda thought about men, she would inevitably compare them to Ahmad Sultan.

It was at this point that Umm Ibrahim changed her tune. She began to carry Ahmad Sultan's greetings to Miss Linda. This astonished Linda at first, since Ahmad Sultan had been on the estate for years without sending her greetings or any kind of word at all. Then, too, the only greeting that moved Linda was Safwat's, and only rarely did she hear from him.

But Umm Ibrahim knew all the tricks. She would deliver the message as if it was spontaneous, without purpose or plan. Then the greetings became deliberate. And one day Umm Ibrahim opened her heart to Linda, and said she had a great secret to tell her that no one — neither human being nor jinn — knew. She would not say a word until she made Linda swear by Christ and the Bible that she would never tell a soul. And Linda repeated the oath to put Umm Ibrahim's heart at ease. Then as breathlessly as a man declaring himself to his sweetheart, Umm Ibrahim told her that Ahmad Sultan was madly in love with her, but without hope or expectations. She herself knew about it only because she went to visit him one day when he was sick, and in a moment of weakness he revealed his secret to her, and then asked her to keep it from everyone, especially Linda. But the bonds of friendship are strong, and friends have certain obligations, and Umm Ibrahim could not imagine herself knowing anything that important and not telling her dear Linda.

That first time Linda laughed until she almost died. Her laughter made Umm Ibrahim's heart uneasily skip a beat, for her greatest fear was that Linda would take the matter as a joke, and all her plans would be destroyed. As a matter of fact, Linda paid little attention, since her dreams were filled with images of Safwat gazing at her with his dear face, and telling her these things. She never expected them to come from Ahmad Sultan, her father's subordinate, who would never be the hero of a young girl's dreams, a girl, that is, of her social class and position.

When Umm Ibrahim sensed this, she changed the subject immediately, and tried neither to argue nor persuade. But the next day she returned to the conversation briefly and indirectly, and in the evening she touched upon it again. Each time she met Linda she described Ahmad Sultan's state, and the burning passion he was made to suffer until Linda knew with complete certainty that Ahmad Sultan loved her. But there was nothing she could do for him, and she said as much to Umm Ibrahim who in turn made no comment, but continued to mention him to her every time they met.

One day, however, she said nothing at all about Ahmad Sultan, which very much surprised Linda. Prompted by curiosity, she cautiously tried to bring up the subject, but Umm Ibrahim did not respond, nor did she mention him. The visit was nearly over, and she had not said a single word about him. She even got ready to leave with the excuse she had not made supper yet, and Abu Ibrahim must have returned home long ago. And she insisted she had to go, while Linda urged her to stay. Then, and only then, did Linda say as though the matter did not concern her, that her father was going to speak to the commissioner about having Ahmad Sultan moved from the house next to theirs. Although Umm Ibrahim knew perfectly well that this was a lie that Linda had invented on the spur of the moment, she smiled when she heard it, gave her dress a slight hitch, and sat back down. A halting, embarrassed conversation ensued as though both of them were too shy to plunge outright into dangerous waters.

The important thing was that Umm Ibrahim now knew that, deep within Linda, curiosity had begun to stir. And she knew that curiosity, once it took hold of a woman, became her lord and master, moving her wherever it willed. Umm Ibrahim proceeded to feed this new master, portraying Ahmad Sultan to Linda over and over in a way that began to disturb her, and to inflame her imagination when she was alone. There were times, however, when she doubted everything, and thought it unlikely that Ahmad Sultan was as deeply in love with her as Umm Ibrahim claimed. During one such attack of doubt, she confronted Umm Ibrahim with this view. The older woman sensed that the time was right, and that Linda was now in a state which allowed her to say, "If you don't believe me, find out for yourself."

"How?"

"Meet him."

"Good heavens!"

Such was Linda's response on that day. Umm Ibrahim did not wish to persuade her for or against, but would remain neutral. She simply assured Linda that if she wanted this meeting, it would take place in total secrecy with not a whisper of it leaking out to anyone. The only thing she had to do was to come to her house on any pretext, and the rest could be left up to her. From that moment Umm Ibrahim never returned to the subject. Even the chats she was accustomed to having with Linda became few and far between, and a conversation would scarcely begin before she ended it. You could see in Linda's eyes thousands of questions, questions that kept her awake nights thinking about Umm Ibrahim's proposal, questions that, lightning-like, flashed from her features. Umm Ibrahim responded only with a sly, practiced disregard. She even stopped coming to Mesiha Afendi's house. A day went by, and then another with no news of her. Her nerves strained to their utmost, Linda sent Dumyaan to inquire, and he returned, saying Umm Ibrahim was deathly sick. She asked her father during lunch for permission to visit her, and being in an expansive mood, he gave it. And she sent Dumyaan to say she would see her after sunset.

So there sat Linda by her side in a dress that exposed her throat and shoulders, and did not succeed in concealing the hair under her arms which showed, in spite of her efforts, thick and yellow. Each time she looked at the room and saw it, neat and tidy, as though made ready for a bridegroom and not just a visitor, Linda felt herself shiver with fear as though afraid what she anticipated would happen. And each time Umm Ibrahim looked at her, and saw the special care she had taken with her toilette as though she were not going to visit a sick woman but had prepared herself for something more, her body shivered, too, her heart pounding with joy, as though it frightened her to have successfully achieved at last what she had striven for so tirelessly.

Some kind of conversation had to take place.

It centered on the discovery of the foundling's mother, and that she was a married woman who became pregnant behind her husband's back. Umm Ibrahim forgot she was supposed to be sick, and sat up to tell Linda stories about the migrant workers and their disgusting lack of morals, how there was no sin or crime they would hesitate to commit, and that without embarrassment or shame as if they weren't human beings at all, but a pack of wild animals. Uneasily, Linda agreed with her, and nodded her head in a troubled way, assuring her at the same time that God would surely forgive them, for they were ignorant, and did not know what they did. Linda insisted on the matter of forgiveness so strongly Umm Ibrahim was made uneasy, and she stopped talking, and changed the subject.

Pointing to the caftan hanging on a clothes rack at the head of the bed, Linda asked about Sheikh Abu Ibrahim. His wife said he had gone to celebrate a religious feast at the Number Six farm. Indeed, had Linda gone up to the roof and listened, she would have seen a kerosene lamp burning far away to the south, and heard Sheikh Abu Ibrahim's voice as he led a rhythmical *thikr** circle in perfect harmony with the prayer leader al-Bur'i in his famous cloak.

The conversation lapsed into silence, a silence that almost lasted too long, all but heightening that air of expectancy and excitement that had dominated the room since Linda came in. Except that it did not last. They heard a knock at the open outer door ... the knock of someone announcing his arrival.

Umm Ibrahim, although perfectly sure of the newcomer's identity, called out in the lingering tones of someone pretending to be sick, "Yes, who is it?"

Linda's face grew pale, her skin started to prickle, and her hair stood practically on end. And Ahmad Sultan entered. His dark tarboosh was tilted so far over his forehead it almost hid the hairs in his right eyebrow. His silk villager's robe was pressed, the black coat

---

*This rite, which is practiced by Sufis, the mystics of Islam, consists of the unceasing repetition of certain words or formulas in praise of God. It is often accompanied by music or dancing — Tr.

92

worn over it, and he himself was clean shaven with his moustache clipped and groomed, and his face shining. With a wide, practiced smile, and as though unaware of Linda's presence, he said, "Good evening, Umm Ibrahim. I heard you were sick. What's wrong?"

In the same artificial tones as before, Umm Ibrahim replied, "Good evening, Ahmad Afendi. It's nothing, really. Seems like I'm miscarrying or something, I don't know. Aren't you going to say hello, Mr. Ahmad?"

With an exaggerated, theatrical gesture, Ahmad turned slightly, raised his eyebrows as though surprised and said, "Good heavens! Miss Linda's here. Why didn't you tell me, Umm Ibrahim? ..."

He made to turn on his heel and leave the room in a show of good manners. Umm Ibrahim's voice rose, however, and insisted he stay, saying, "Are you a stranger? No one's a stranger but the Devil." During all this, Linda sat where she was as though caught in a whirlpool. She was unable to look in Ahmad Sultan's direction, or at Umm Ibrahim; she couldn't even focus on the ceiling or the floor. Ahmad Sultan seemed to have responded to Umm Ibrahim's persistence, for he cleared his throat, came a few steps forward, and said haltingly, "Now I know why the house looks so radiant. ... Good evening, Miss Linda."

A heavy silence prevailed. Linda moved her lips, wanting to answer him, but nothing came out. Umm Ibrahim saved the situation by saying, "And a good evening to you, dear! May God keep you strong, and give you everything your heart desires. ..."

Ahmad Sultan held out his hand to greet Linda. She was flustered momentarily, not knowing what to do. At last she found that the best thing she could do was to put out her hand, and greet him. Their hands touched for only a moment, but what a moment ... Ahmad Sultan's hand with its large, hairy, hard, and experienced fingers, a hand that knew how to soothe a young girl and take her by assuring her that that was the last thing it wanted, this hand reached out and engulfed Linda's, a soft, trembling, tender-skinned, long-fingered hand, hand of the fruit that had ripened on the tree until it was almost too late, that having ripened, had hung there until it nearly fell from the branch of its own accord without being picked, a hand that, as soon as it met Ahmad Sultan's, experienced the hard earth of reality, a reality that it hated but in which it lived, a reality that was bread in the hand, unmistakably more beautiful and more splendid than meat that was seen only in imagination. And Safwat was imagination. As for the man Ahmad Sultan, here was his hand, unknown to her and to her imagination but exuding virility, a virility which stirred things

93

deep within her that had never been moved before.

The greeting lasted no more than a moment, but that was time enough for Linda's small palm to become damp, and when she took her hand from his, tiny beads of sweat trickled down.

*　　　　　*　　　　　*

Not far away over the stone bridge in the house of Commissioner Fikri Afendi, his son Safwat tried to sleep, and couldn't. Failing that, he pretended to be asleep, since he knew an enormous catastrophe was about to befall him. The drone of conversation reached him across the darkened hall from the sitting room, the room where his father had admitted Mesiha Afendi a short while before, astonished by the unexpected visit at that hour of the night.

But by now his amazement must have ended, for a low-voiced murmuring reached him, and the only sounds he heard were Mesiha Afendi's voice talking non-stop, and his father's cough as he listened without speaking. And then there was silence — he must be showing him the letter. The hell with him, the letter, and the day he talked about Linda to Ahmad Sultan, the day they found the bastard. ...

After the conversation with Ahmad, his emotions had run riot, and he was seized by a wild impulse urging him that now was the time to tell Linda everything in his heart.

For two whole days he thought about it. Then he wrote that damned letter after tearing up dozens of drafts that didn't satisfy him. The letter stayed in his pocket for another two days, while he hesitated, partly over whether to send it, and partly because he couldn't figure out how. ...

Then he thought of Mahboob who, rumor had it, was the messenger for their love letters. Why shouldn't he use him? At first Mahboob pretended not to understand; then realizing that wouldn't wash, he was nervous and afraid, saying he'd sworn since the day he found his wife's letter that he'd never carry anything like that again. But Safwat continued alternately to threaten and cajole, and gave him twenty piasters on the spot. Clearly, Mahboob agreed, but he repeated he was afraid he'd be caught with the letter and there'd be hell to pay. So Safwat swore he would be fully responsible should anything happen.

Safwat never knew whether Mahboob's consenting to deliver the letter was a generous impulse that sprang from the heart, or whether it concealed the most malicious intention. Nor did he ever know if it was just plain naivete that made Mahboob go to Mesiha Afendi's house, and ask for Miss Linda out of a clear blue sky, so that his question attracted the attention of Mesiha Afendi himself who collared him, searched him, and found the letter as easy as you please. Was it simpleness on Mahboob's part, or was it spite, the cunning malice of that short, beardless man who, refusing to play the role of a lovers' go-between for some reason known only to himself, had deliberately revealed his purpose to Mesiha Afendi? All he had to do after they found the letter on him was to say, "It's none of my doing, anyway. ... It was Mr. Safwat Bey who told me to. I'd do anything for the commissioner."

If only that were all that was wrong—, if only the letter had been the sole disaster. The biggest calamity of all was that Safwat, seized by an intense anxiety over his plan, began to watch Mesiha Afendi's house from the moment he handed Mahboob the letter. But he was not to be permitted to see Mahboob enter the house, since a little after sunset he was startled by the sight of Linda herself — all dressed up — coming out. At first he thought she was going to their house for some reason. But she did not cross the stone bridge, nor did she take the path to their house, but turned off in the direction of the farm. He followed her at a distance, speculating on her destination. He was not given the opportunity for long, however, since in no time he found she was knocking on the door of Sheikh Abu Ibrahim's house and entering. What on earth would she be doing there? The question nagged at him for a long time without his finding an answer. Finally he convinced himself that she must be visiting Umm Ibrahim.

Here his face began to light up, and a crazy idea took hold of him. Sheikh Abu Ibrahim was at the Number Six farm celebrating a feast, and Linda was now sitting alone with his wife. Wasn't this, unexpected as it was, a heaven-sent opportunity? What would happen if he were to go into Sheikh Abu Ibrahim's house right now, pretending he was asking for him, for example, or pretending he wanted to talk about some private matter? Their discussions were well known, since they often spent a large part of the evening at the bridge or in front of Junaidi's store, debating the eternal questions of God's existence, free will, and predestination, Sheikh Abu Ibrahim listening to his doubts and uncertainties with a kind and tolerant heart as the discussion lengthened and they were still far from agreement. Why not pretend to ask for him, and go in, and if Umm Ibrahim invited him, sit down? Some kind of conversation must take place, and he would surely find a chance to be alone with Linda, and to tell her what lay hidden in his heart. Maybe he could even walk her home.

Despite the soundness of the plan, Safwat hesitated. From time to time he moved a few steps toward the house only to stop in each instance as his courage deserted him. He was mortified at the same time, because the spot where he stood was in plain sight of passersby who greeted him, and wondered what he was doing. The matter did require careful thought, for his ability to face Linda had been greatly impaired from the moment he decided to declare his love. Accordingly, Safwat withdrew, choosing a corner of the street next to a grain silo whose huge bulk all but hid him from view. Greatly disturbed, he proceeded to bite his nails and mull the situation over. While he was so occupied, he spied Ahmad Afendi Sultan, unmistakable in his tarboosh and overcoat, coming down the street. Shrinking nearer to the wall, Safwat hid himself behind the silo, not wanting the other man to see him and ridicule him for many evenings to come. But the strange thing was that Ahmad Sultan did not pass him, but turned before he was halfway down the street. He knocked on Sheikh Abu Ibrahim's open door, and went in. Safwat's violently pounding heart made a similar sound, and he was nearly blinded by the great confusion that came over him. But it wasn't long before he managed to observe the door, the sheikh's door, being moved from within by a feminine hand, and then it quickly swung shut. The blood rose in a hot fountain to his head. He left his hiding place and hurried toward the canal, out of breath and disoriented, like someone just bitten by a poisonous snake.

A thousand things went through his mind in that moment.

He thought of going to get his gun, storming the house, and shooting them on the spot. He thought of saying nothing and waiting, since it might be a coincidence. He thought of going and knocking on the door with the excuse he was looking for Sheikh Abu Ibrahim, surprising them with his appearance. He thought of every possibility, but with each new scenario he found himself unable to act as though his will had been struck by a sudden paralysis, and all it could do was weep. But he refused to give in and do that. All at once he found his only concern was to find Mahboob and take the letter from him before he went off with it, since it was no longer necessary, and since goddamned letters were no good, anyway.

But he did not find Mahboob. In vain he tried to locate him as though every one of his life's goals had crystallized into that one thing: finding Mahboob. When he failed at that, too, he felt that now he did want to cry. And so he went home and collapsed on his bed. But this time tears eluded him, and he continued to lie there with his eyes open like a lunatic. Until he heard a knock at their door, and

Mesiha Afendi asking to see his father on urgent business, and his father getting out of bed to open up the sitting room for the chief clerk. With his own ears he heard Mesiha tell his father the story of what happened when Mahboob came to ask for Miss Linda. And in a little while his father would come and call him to account.

Safwat went on lying there, his eyes wide open, as he waited for the well-known footsteps of his father to approach. He was ready to face him, as though it no longer mattered whether he was taken to task, or of what he was accused. But when his father's footsteps drew near, Safwat found himself closing his eyes and pretending to be asleep. His father, the lamp in his hand, stood at the door to his room a long time as though undecided whether to wake him, or to leave his reckoning and punishment for the morning.

In the end he appeared to settle upon the latter course, for tomorrow would be a new day.

*   *   *

But Fikri Afendi was unable to call Safwat to account in the morning, since when he and Umm Safwat woke up, they couldn't find him. What they found was a letter from him, saying he had gone to look for work in Cairo during vacation, far from them and the estate, and he saw no point in discussing it with them since they were sure to object. The letter also said he was sorry that he'd been forced to "borrow" all the money in his mother's purse, but he promised to pay it back when he received his first month's pay. The funny thing was that the paper on which he wrote the letter seemed to have been a rough draft of the letter to Linda, since the words "my darling" were written several times on the back and crossed out. Fikri Afendi read the letter twice, and then tore it up, trying to conceal his satisfaction at Safwat's escape. Actually, Safwat had done him a favor by relieving him of the need to confront his son and make him answer to the charge, always a difficult, troublesome task as far as Fikri Afendi was concerned, which caused him greater pain than it did Safwat.

CHAPTER SEVENTEEN

A second shelter was put up for Aziza close to Old Mother Migrant, there being no further need for her to go to the field every day with the laborers now that the commissioner knew all about her, and agreed to go on paying her wages while she lay ill.

The shelter and the sick woman lying under it were guaranteed to attract attention, and anyone who did not yet know Aziza's story was soon acquainted with it. In truth, the estate inhabitants' behavior toward Aziza was very strange. At first they were concerned only with proving that the culprit was a migrant. Once that fact was established and they felt themselves secure, their curiosity drove them to find out everything they could about her. When they had done that, and it was rumored that the woman was so sick that she lay prostrate in the migrant camp, all that mattered to them was the chance to look at her and see what she was like. For that purpose they came to the campsite singly and in groups, men, women, even youngsters, and infants. Everyone who came to look at Aziza pretended to be on the way to the threshing floor, the irrigation machine, or the field. When he saw the shelter, he would hesitate as if the sight of it had made him stop. Then he would go and ask about it as though knowing nothing, and he would stare at the sleeping woman for a long, long time.

That was what happened in the beginning. As time passed, however, there was no further need for pretense. Anyone who wanted to look at Aziza stood openly not far from where she lay, and waited for her to turn, make a sound, or show her face. After they began to take the presence of the Gharabwa for granted, if they were there, they would stand around and watch Aziza even in front of them. They did that without exchanging a word with her fellow-villagers as though they had no connection with them whatsoever, and as though Aziza was no longer one of them, but a public spectacle that everyone had the right to see. And the Gharabwa accepted the situation with considerable tolerance and self-control.

Yet, when Aziza became delirious and began to cry out from the fever, and her fellow-villagers rushed to talk to her, comfort her, and pat her reassuringly as if she was completely rational and knew what she was saying, when she began to do that, the ice was broken. The onlookers from the farm began to speak freely with the Gharabwa, and joined in with a word of sympathy, or bit their lips in common anxiety. One word would lead to another, and in this way a conversation would start between the two groups of men and the two groups of women.

But three days after Aziza had allowed herself to rest, she began to have convulsions. Her body stiffened until it became dry and rigid as a stick, and she bit her tongue until it bled. Before such a sight, the farm people were unable to keep themselves from hurrying to her side as did the migrant workers from her village, helping to force open her mouth, massage her body, and make her inhale onion juice.

The convulsions left Aziza prey to fits of sudden terror. She would leap suddenly out of bed, screaming, and run to the nearby canal and throw herself in, fully clothed, as though wanting to put out a fire burning inside her. Then the farm people would help the migrant workers pull her from the water, carry her to the shelter, and put her to bed. At such times they sat at her side in groups made up of Gharabwa and farm residents, groups which, when Aziza had been calmed and they were reassured she was no worse, would go on to talk among themselves. The conversation would start with Aziza and her condition, and would end with each person speaking of himself and his concerns.

How quickly did the change in their attitude affect even the way they talked about Aziza! After having circulated her story among themselves, all but nauseated by her, the tale, and the Gharabwa in general, the inhabitants of the estate began to give it short shrift, abbreviating the tale as though it had become shameful, or as though to dwell on it showed disrespect to a lady and offended people's honor. Even those who went to the camp with the sole purpose of gawking at Aziza grew fewer in number until they all but disappeared.

When Aziza grew worse, they joined forces to look for medicine in every house and on every farm, and Junaidi gave her a bottle of vinegar at half-price. Nabawiya, on behalf of herself and her children as she said, slaughtered a small rabbit for her which she cooked and brought in its pot for Old Mother Migrant to feed her. This she did amid the amazement of the farm people who felt that was too much to expect from poor, destitute Nabawiya. But she did it with the noblest of motives. Nor was her nobility diminished by the fact that, when the pot was returned, she scoured it with earth and mud, and spoke the Muslim creed over it seven times before using it again.*

Thus it was around the shelter and Aziza's sick bed that the farm people and the migrant workers became acquainted. It was a reserved and limited association at first, but through it the farm people discovered that the migrant workers had villages, too, and that like them they knew about farming and worked the land. They also had houses, relatives, and aunts on both sides of the family. Likewise, they disagreed and fought among themselves, and had complaints about their boss, and reasons to complain about the commissioner, the administration and the estate.

So, too, did the farm children begin to play openly with the migrant children, and their fathers did not forbid them, but only advised them not to let the migrant children breathe in their faces, since it was likely their breath carried germs.

Fikri Afendi, in the meantime, was extremely anxious about his son, even though it was not the first time Safwat had left them and gone to Cairo, claiming to be looking for work during vacation. He wanted only to reassure himself of his son's whereabouts, since the money he had taken was not enough, and he would have to send him more.

But in spite of this greater anxiety of his, he was also concerned about Aziza. He himself did not know why ever since he found her he had felt as if he were responsible for her — as though he had gone looking for her for that very reason. On his way to the field, he would pass the place where she lay, and do nothing more than stand at her head, and look down at her as she moved restlessly on her bed of straw, and mumbled a few incoherent words. He would stand like that for a time, and then leave her, his heart troubled. There was nothing else he could do. It was too risky to have the county doctor examine her, or to send her to the fever hospital since someone might discover that she was the mother and, subsequently, the

---

*This description refers to a purification ritual performed by certain Muslims following contact with a substance that is considered unclean. According to the Shafitic school of theology, there are three degrees of impurity (najasa) of which the third and most extreme (al-ghaliza) calls for the stringent measures described in the text. The contaminated object is cleaned seven times (once with earth) if a pig or a dog has licked it or otherwise polluted it. The author clearly intends this allusion to describe the extent of the peasants' ingrained revulsion to the Gharabwa despite the fact that the two groups have begun to associate with one another — Tr.

murderess. That would be disastrous not only for her, but for him, as well, considering he knew about the matter, had concealed it, and failed to notify the proper authorities. All he could do was to order Usta Zaki, the estate barber, who also occupied the position of barber-surgeon for the county while simultaneously pursuing the trades of cutting hair, circumcising children, and prescribing medicines to strengthen sexual potency, rejuvenate the old, and cure fevers, to order him in secret as if afraid to have anyone catch him in a moment of weakness and compassion, to take charge of Aziza's treatment since he would personally see to the bill. And, although Usta Zaki did in fact take over her treatment, in the white turban he wore over a white skullcap, his face clean shaven, and a gold tooth flashing in his mouth, in spite of his taking charge of the case, her condition became if anything, worse. The incidents of her throwing herself in the canal were repeated, and at that point Fikri Afendi ordered Arafa to see that her neighbor Umm al-Hasan stayed with her, and did not go to the field though she would collect her daily pay just the same.

There was something else that no one ever knew. The friendship between Chief Clerk Mesiha Afendi and Commissioner Fikri Afendi was over for good, and the letter that Mesiha intercepted did nothing but make matters worse. Of his own accord, Mesiha waited for a chance to catch the commissioner in a mistake so he could write a complaint against him, which would be copied by Sheikh Abu Ibrahim and sent to the Cairo office under an assumed name. Mesiha Afendi found just the opportunity he was looking for — come down to him from the wide gates of heaven — in the fact that daily wages for Aziza and her neighbor were being recorded. After he checked with Ahmad Sultan that the two were indeed registered in the daily pay roster, he stayed up an entire night to write a long memorandum to that effect in which he accused the commissioner of having exaggerated the number of laborers and divided the difference with the contractor, and of having falsified the daily wage register, and that the witness to all this was alive and present, and the only thing the Right Honorable Khawaaga had to do was to send the inspector to investigate the above.

After Mesiha Afendi was satisfied with the language of the complaint, he slipped it inside his pillowcase, ready to give it to Sheikh Abu Ibrahim to be copied and sent out in the morning.

When the chief clerk at last lay down to rest, the memorandum in the pillowcase under his head, he found himself becoming troubled over whether to send it. Why? He didn't know. He had never been reluctant to send a complaint before, why should he shilly-shally now? Why did he feel ashamed as an image of the shelter, Aziza lying beneath it, came to mind, and her screams and delirious ravings, besieging him from all sides and calling him, rang in his ears?

The next morning when he awoke he hesitated whether to take the complaint in or leave it behind. In the end his indecision led him to ask Dumyaan. Without letting his brother know what was on his mind, he asked, "Should I take it or leave it?"

Dumyaan wet two fingers, rolled down his sleeve, lifted his face to the ceiling and said, "Leave it, brother, and God will make everything easy for you."

The complaint stayed folded in the pillowcase.

*   *   *

Aziza went on lying in that unshaded spot exposed continually to the heat of the sun. The thin roof of the shelter, riddled with holes, was unsuccessful in driving back the blazing heat, and neither the vinegar, nor the massage, nor the treatment of Usta Zaki the barber helped her. She continued to lie there, the fever buzzing in her body so loudly that Umm al-Hasan could almost hear it, and feel it when she held her hand. Flies swarmed around her, she was covered with sweat, and her spells of unconsciousness became longer and deeper. At last her delirious ravings turned into screams. If she regained consciousness, she would scarcely open her eyes, at which Umm al-Hasan would say, "How are you feeling now, dear?" then she would beat her breast and cry out, "Oh, my God!" Then she would hit her cheeks repeatedly, and tear at her clothes and flesh with her nails in spite of all the efforts her neighbor and passersby made to calm her and bind her hands. Such attempts to subdue her did nothing but increase her rage and rebellion, and she would not stop clawing at herself until she once again sank into the subterranean passages of unconsciousness.

No longer was the shelter a mark of Gharabwa shame to be hidden from sight. For, once the story became public knowledge and every detail was known, nothing remained for the Gharabwa to be ashamed of. It became — like their language, their poverty, and their need — something they did not try to conceal. So, too, the people of the estate, those same men and women who once told her story in secret, feeling they discussed a forbidden, shameful thing, now talked about it openly as though it had ceased to be shocking. They were no longer concerned with Aziza's story, but with Aziza herself, mad, sick Aziza who was in torment. Their change of attitude even extended to the shelter where she lay, as though it were now a shrine and she, a holy woman. It became impossible for anyone to pass the structure without looking at it, not out of curiosity or satisfaction, but with sympathy and fellow-feeling, the look of a person who wished he could do something to ease the suffering of that poor, feverish creature.

Everyone became worried about Aziza. Meanwhile, Aziza herself became a savage beast, out of her mind when she was awake, and a rigid corpse whose only link to life was the morbid fever that rose in waves from her body when she lost consciousness.

Until the tenth day.

Right from the beginning, Umm al-Hasan awoke to find Aziza showing signs of improvement. Her temperature was down, her eyes were open, conscious and rational, and her breathing, though coming and going slowly in her chest, was deep and even. In the forenoon, Aziza's lips parted, but Umm al-Hasan, though she listened intently, was unable to make out the words. Finally, and after much effort, she understood Aziza was saying she wanted something to drink. In anxious haste, Umm al-Hasan got up, brought a cup of water from her jug, and held it close to her lips. Aziza drank it slowly, but she drained every drop. Umm al-Hasan asked if she wanted more, and Aziza's mouth opened, and she said clearly this time, "Yes." Umm al-Hasan ran and brought a second cup, and Aziza drank that, too. Not long afterwards she closed her eyes, and it seemed she would have at last the rest she had been deprived of so long.

An overwhelming joy flooded Umm al-Hasan's heart as, feeling Aziza's forehead, she found her temperature was back to normal and she was sleeping, her extreme pallor almost the only clue to how sick she had been.

At noon, high noon, that time of day when life comes to a standstill, and people go home to a lunch that abandons them to a nap from which they do not awake until the coolness of late afternoon, at noon Aziza opened her eyes as suddenly as though she had not slept, her lips parted, and she said something. Umm al-Hasan, understanding she wanted to drink, asked Arafa's young son to go and fill a cup from their water jug, since hers was dry, and the boy went off with the empty cup. In the same instant, Umm al-Hasan was startled to see Aziza tense and suddenly sit up, and to hear her begin to scream, one loud, piercing scream after another. Before Umm al-Hasan could understand what was happening, Aziza had stood up, bringing down the shelter, and begun to run screaming toward the canal. Without conscious thought, Umm al-Hasan went after her, running and screaming, too, and calling for help, afraid Aziza meant to throw herself in the canal again. Hearing her screams, people came from everywhere — the farm, the threshing floor, down off the threshing machine—, alarmed, they came to see what was wrong. "Stop her, she's going to throw herself in the canal!" cried Umm al-Hasan. And everyone ran to try and stop her, but she turned on them, biting, kicking, and clawing like a wild, demented creature, and all they could do was retreat. She did not, however, throw herself in the canal. She started to run again until she reached the place in which they had found the baby, where traces of dried, black blood still remained.

Amid the astonishment and bewilderment of those gathered around her, Aziza squatted down on the canal bank as though preparing herself to give birth. Screams tore from her, one scream following another, as though she were going into labor. Then with her hand she groped until she found the half-burnt stick of willow that still lay on the bank. She bit down on the stick, and her body took on a look of frenzied fear as she bit harder and ground her teeth. Savagely she continued the pressure and increased it, biting harder and harder, snarling like a wild animal, as the blood flowed from her mouth and teeth, and stained the branch. Her eyes were flaming coals, her hair was matted and unkempt as a jinn's, and her hands squeezed the canal mud until it was dry dirt clods. Then suddenly as though something burst inside her she fell, and lay motionless on the bank of the canal.

All this took no more than a few minutes. Everyone was shocked and bewildered, frozen in place by what was happening. No one moved until Aziza collapsed, and when they ran to feel her pulse, they found she was dead.

A low, fervent prayer arose from the lips of the men, "There is no strength or refuge save in God, in Him alone is our refuge and our strength," and the few women who were present sobbed out loud. Umm al-Hasan shed painful tears as she tried, with the men's help, to free the willow stick from the lifeless jaws.

The boss's young son who had brought the tin cup full of water for Aziza to drink, returned with it to their hut. But a short while later, he came to a stop, turned toward the canal, and threw the cup in. It was not long before the sound of his crying rose on the air.

*   *   *

104

Word did not reach the migrant workers in the field until after lunch. Neither the efforts of the boss nor those of the estate overseers could stop what happened when they heard. Unrest spread through their long line, and when the cane sticks were cracked on their backs, ordering them to go back to work, those backs straightened for the first time, and the men turned to face the overseers and foremen with unblinking, wide-open eyes, and faces that warned of a revolt whose measure God alone knew—the revolt of the silent ones who had been silent and patient too long. Strangely enough, when the overseers and foremen saw those faces, they changed their ways immediately. They stopped the insults and sticks, and started in with entreaties and tricks, saying their livelihood depended on what happened, and they were poor men with families to support.

Work was over for the migrant laborers more than an hour before the usual time that day, and they returned to camp, racing each other along the paths in their haste for the road to end.

That evening the migrant camp behind the stable teemed with an unprecedented number of people. The peasants from the big farm and the other farms had come with some of their womenfolk to offer condolences to the migrant workers, man to man, and equal to equal. Aziza had been laid in the place recently occupied by the shelter. She was covered with one of the cotton sacks used when they shook the plants for worms. Around her were gathered the migrant women and those farm women who had come to share their sorrow. Some cried silently, while others eulogized Aziza, and lamented her dying in the land of exile far away from home and family. Still others took part in the kind of conversation that women enjoy only at funerals: the farm woman telling the migrant woman — or it might have been the reverse — about her unhappy change of fortune, her bad luck with a neglectful husband, her dress that was so torn and full of holes that it wouldn't hold a handful of salt, her troublesome children, and her daughter pursued by a suitor with two whole *feddans*.

Not far away in the foreground of the threshing floor, the migrant men sat receiving the condolences of the men from the estate. Turbans mingled with turbans, and *gallabiyas* with *gallabiyas*, and you could no longer tell the peasant from the migrant worker, nor the bereaved from the man who came to condole. Meanwhile, Sheikh Abu Ibrahim, the Quran-reciter, had occupied the seat of one of the threshing sleds that stood on a half-threshed pile of wheat and proceeded to recite in his hoarse, rasping voice what he could in

105

the time allowed from "Surat-al-Nisa,"* while the sun's disk reddened and set behind the huge mountain of straw left over by the machine.

Unlike everyone else, Dumyaan at that moment was hovering near the commissioner's house, without a basket on his arm this time, waiting in the hope that Umm Safwat would look down from the balcony and talk to him. She did not, however, since she was sitt- on the living-room couch, a migrant girl seated before her on the floor, who massaged her feet, and told her about Aziza and her husband, and the way they all lived in the village.

Dumyaan continued to circle the house, hesitating, until he grew bold enough to go in by the back door that led to the courtyard and the kitchen. He entered, shouting, "Umm Safwat ... Umm Safwat ... Don't you want me to tell your fortune?"

Though he shouted as he always did in his reedy voice that sounded like an adolescent boy's, he felt at that moment a strange trembling in the voice and in himself.

Minutes later Dumyaan left the commissioner's house by the front door — thrown out, this time, and roundly cursed. Aimlessly he continued to walk until he reached the threshing floor and the large group of people that were gathered there. He hesitated a while between going to where the men sat, or joining the women gathered around Aziza in the migrants' camp. It would appear he was afraid of the men, since before long he made his way toward the cluster of women. And that day Dumyaan shed such agonized tears that he nearly made the women laugh.

Commissioner Fikri Afendi and the men with him — Mesiha Afendi, Ahmad Sultan, Usta Muhammad, Sheikh Abd al-Waarith al-Kabir, the storehouse keeper, and the chief overseer — were sitting on some ancient chairs, most of them having lost their plaited palm-leaf seats, in front of the administration buildings. Their get-together was observed from a distance by some of the peasants who took pleasure in being uninvited guests, picking up stray bits of information, and learning everything they could about what took place on the estate. The commissioner, along with the men assembled around him, was carefully studying the solution he had reached in the matter of Aziza. For, by her death Aziza had created a problem for him that he had not thought of before. He could not report her death or burial on the estate, since a report would require that an autopsy be performed, and who knew where that would lead

---

*The Quran, Chapter IV, "Women" — Tr.

— charges of concealing a criminal, an inquest, an investigation. There was no answer but to send the body back to the migrants' village. There Hagg Abd al-Rahim, the contractor for the migrants, would take charge, since he was responsible first and last for the laborers and their lives, and he must be accountable in case of their deaths, too. He would be able to make some kind of deal with the village mayor, who was a friend and relative, to report her death as if she hadn't been with the migrant workers, or had been with them, but returned home when she got sick and died in her village. He could do whatever he wanted as long as it freed the estate and the commissioner of responsibility. Whatever he wanted — but the main thing was to get Aziza's body back to her village, especially since Arafa and the other laborers were determined she should be buried there, feeling that to bury her as a stranger in the estate cemetery would be an unpardonable insult to themselves and their traditions.

But how to move the body was a problem, and it had perplexed Fikri Afendi for a long time until he figured out the solution. The answer lay in the estate truck, which went to the migrants' village every fifteen days to bring them their supplies of Gharabwa bread, cheese, onions, lentils, and whey. Although the truck was not scheduled to leave for a few days yet, it wouldn't be too risky to let it go early.

The commissioner had sent for Usta Abdu the truck driver, and he began to give him his instructions in a solemn voice that was meant to be commanding. His tone did not permit the driver to make excuses, or shirk his duty, giving him to understand his mission and what he had to do. Usta Abdu showed some reluctance, and raised a few objections, all of which old Usta Muhammad took it upon himself to answer. Final agreement did not appear on Usta Abdu's face until the commissioner promised he would be completely responsible should anything, God forbid, happen. Only then did Usta Abdu send home the high, woolen cap and the *gallabiya* that he usually wore, and ask his wife to bring him the khaki uniform he put on whenever he traveled. Then he went to the garage to get the truck ready for the long trip he had to make over punishing, unpaved roads to stay as far as he could from the kiosks of the highway police.

By the time the truck was ready and everything was prepared, darkness had fallen, and it was time for the migrant laborers to go to the field. The cotton worm eggs had hatched on the Number Ten farm, and the laborers toiled by day, picking off the eggs by hand, and then went at night — in return for a second wage — to shake the worms from the cotton plants, the worms that hid inside cracks in the ground during the day, and began their destructive march only at night.

The shaking operation took place amid the bright lights of the kerosene pressure lanterns, and the laborers preferred it. The work took place at night when the weather was pleasant and cool, and there were songs, and brilliant lantern light, as well as shadows that let them loaf a little and sometimes allowed a rough hand to reach out to its neighbor, and permitted the neighbor, too, to pretend that nothing had happened and say nothing.

The laborers were happy to work at night in spite of everything, in spite of also working during the day and sleeping only the few short hours that were stolen at sunrise and sunset. But the work paid a double wage, and having an exhausted body was no problem. The problem was having a piaster, and getting the heaven-sent opportunity to track one down.

The time came for the laborers to go to the field, but they refused, unwilling to move, until they had said their final good-byes to Aziza.

And the moment when Aziza had to leave drew near. The truck was brought around, roaring, as Usta Abdu backed it up, scolding and cursing the children who hung from its sides, to get as close as possible to where Aziza lay. In gloomy silence the men stood crowded around the truck. Scarcely did the women start to wail than the commissioner jumped at them with a demand for total silence, and a threat to break the neck of anyone who opened her mouth, for the operation must take place quietly, without fuss or scandal.

By the faint light of Junaidi's lantern that several times sputtered and dimmed, Aziza was wrapped in the sack that had covered her. Sheikh Abd al-Waarith donated a worn-out mat that was folded over the sack. Then the body was carried, shrouded in the mat, amid the sobbing of the women and the sorrowful silence of the men, and laid gently on the wooden floor of the truck. All the migrants' empty baskets, jugs and jars were collected, each one marked to identify its owner, and piled on top of the body to hide its outlines. Then Arafa climbed into the truck, accompanied by some of the migrant men. A scream went up from Umm al-Hasan, who demanded to go along, because the deceased was a woman and they were all men, and no one could watch over Aziza better than she. Nor would she be silent until they carried her bodily to the truck and set her down. Abd al-Muttalib also insisted on going with them to escort Aziza to her final resting place, saying he couldn't let Usta Abdu go off alone on such a perilous mission.

At last Commissioner Fikri Afendi, breathing unsteadily, said to

Abdu, "Put your faith in God, Usta, and get moving."

Shifting gears, Usta Abdu replied, "We're on our way. ... The Faatiha*. ..."

The truck pulled out, the sound of its motor rising from among the hundreds of men and women assembled there, whose faces, drained of blood, were lit only by Junaidi's dim lantern. Some of them, in spite of themselves, were unable to keep from saying, "Good-bye, Aziza ... good-bye. ..."

A short while later the truck had straightened out on the agricultural highway that ran parallel to the Delta line. Silent and morose, the driver smoked the cigarette that Arafa had pressed on him, while at his side sat Abd al-Muttalib, likewise grim and unspeaking. Those in the back of the truck held fast to the side as though avoiding sharp needles. Each time the truck gave a jolt, they hung on more tightly, trying to keep as far away as they could from the pile of baskets and jars that covered the deceased.

As the truck whined and swayed under its load, and the subdued humming noise it made was borne on the winds and slowly absorbed into the huge masses of darkness crouching on the breast of creation, the line of laborers shaking the worms had formed under the light from lanterns hung on long branches, and bamboo sticks began to rise and fall on the bent-over backs, while the voices of the overseers and foremen shouted in an unceasing cadence, "Get down lower, boy ... lower, girl."

---

*The Faatiha ("The Opening"), which is the first chapter of the Quran, is recited before all important undertakings:

    In the Name of Allah, the Merciful, the Compassionate.

    1. Praise belongs to Allah, the Lord of the worlds,
    2. The Merciful, the Compassionate.
    3. Wielder of the Day of Judgment.
    4. Thee do we serve, and on Thee do we call for help;
    5. Guide us the straight path,
    6. The path of those upon whom Thou has bestowed good,
    7. Not (that) of those upon whom anger falls, or those who go astray.

Bell, p. 1 — Tr.

EPILOGUE

The year came to an end. Despite everything, Fikri Afendi's efforts were crowned with success, and though the cotton worm hatched, it was vanquished. The crop was saved, and the Gharabwa returned to their villages.

When the next year came, and with it the Gharabwa, the peasants still remembered part of Aziza's story and her tragic end. But the barrier that had stood between them and the migrant workers was gone forever. It became routine for the migrant men to spend evenings with the farm people in their homes, and for their women to visit each other. Over and above that, Salim Abu Zaid, a stable hand on the estate, even married a Gharabwa girl who caught his eye. He proposed to her, and when she returned to her village at the end of the season, he went, too, with a group of peasants from the estate, to ask her family for her hand, and bring her back his bride.

The next year did not see Fikri Afendi as estate commissioner. As it turned out, Khawaaga Zaghib had sold the estate to the Belgian company, which appointed a commissioner who looked like one of its own foreigners (even if afterwards it became known that he was a Turk and a Muslim, he looked and acted just like a foreigner). But the company and the new commissioner did not stay long, either, since the company soon sold the land to al-Ahmadi Pasha when he offered the right price at a profit of thousands of pounds. The pasha converted the system of temporary sharecropping that had prevailed on the estate to a rental system. The peasants signed blank leases, and he wrote in the stipulations he wanted.

It did not surprise anyone to wake up one morning and find Ahmad Afendi Sultan had resigned his job and left the estate. It was said he took a clerical position in the office of a mixed courts' lawyer in Tanta. No one was surprised, for everyone knew that Ahmad Sultan had always been unhappy with his work on the estate, regarding himself to be squandering his life and his youth there dirt-cheap. Everyone was, however, truly astonished when one day Miss Linda disappeared, and Mesiha Afendi nearly lost his mind as he searched here, there and everywhere for some sign of her. Everyone's amazement subsided, and the secret was revealed when it was learned that she went off to marry Ahmad Sultan, that the marriage took place in a police station, and that his resignation, her disappearance and eveything else happened by mutual consent. The

episode added dozens of years to Mesiha Afendi's appearance. Most of his hair turned white, and he no longer cared about the cleanliness of his clothing or the placing of handkerchiefs under his collar to protect it from sweat. He severed all ties with Linda and her husband, and swore that he, his sons and his wife would never acknowledge her, see her, or speak of her again. But the passage of the days — ah, those days — soon made him forget and forgive. He replied to the many letters Linda sent him every week with a single communication, grave and tersely worded but beginning with the salutation, "Our dear daughter Linda. ..."

The years continued to witness differences of a new kind flare up between the peasants, who were now tenants, and al-Ahmadi Pasha — courts, bailiffs, sequestrations, guards on the livestock and movable property, forced sales by public auction, and incidents of arson in the estate's water wheels, machinery, and crops.

112

Then came the revolution, and the Agricultural Reform Law was issued. Al-Ahmadi Pasha sold the land to the peasants (so the law would not apply to him)* along with everything else that went with the estate — livestock, riding animals, threshing and irrigation machines, and tractors. He even razed the mansion and the enormous storehouses and sold the rubble. Nor did he have need of all the employees, overseers, *ustas*, and laborers. Some left the estate for good, and some became peasants and bought land. The only one who remained as an employee was Mesiha Afendi whom al-Ahmadi Pasha's office designated to take over the accounts for the two hundred *feddans* left in the pasha's name.

The landmarks of the estate were completely changed, for there were no mansion, no stables, no administration, no commissioner, no inspector, and no workmen, guards, or day laborers. But a new society came into being. Hundreds of small (nominal)** "landowners"*** living in the same houses they occupied as tenant farmers and peasants, hundreds of small folk, some of whom began to grow bigger, become rich and hire laborers, while others grew smaller, became poorer, and put themselves out for hire.

Years passed, and change followed upon change. Naturally, the migrant workers no longer came to the estate, and everyone completely forgot about them and about Aziza. ...

All that remained of them and of her was a willow tree that stands today beside the canal which time has not altered. It is said that it sprang from the stick which they took from Aziza when she died. Forgotten and trodden in the mud, it sprouted and grew to become that tree. Strangest of all, to this day people consider it a blessed tree, and its leaves are still widely regarded by the women of the area as a tried and proven cure for childlessness.

---

*The parenthetical expression above was added by the author to the 1977 edition of *al-Haram* printed by Dar Gharib. It is not found in Dar al-Hilal's 1965 edition — Tr.

**See preceding footnote — Tr.

***Quotation marks have been used to indicate the author's 1977 parenthetical expression: (landowners). This, along with the two preceding footnotes, indicates Idris's disenchantment with the results of land reform — Tr.

BIOGRAPHIC NOTES

Yusuf Idris was born in 1927 in an Egyptian village. He studied medicine and was in practice for a time, later becoming a government health inspector. Though he has written novels and is a playwright of great originality, it is as a short story writer that he is best known in the Arab world. He is essentially a political writer and brings to his stories a unique ability to exploit both the classical and colloquial languages to his literary purposes. Much of his work has been translated into Russian and other Eastern European languages.

Kristin Peterson-Ishaq is a graduate of Georgetown University and has an M.A. in Arabic language and literature from the American University in Cairo. She has taught at the University of Vermont and currently resides in Essex, Vermont.

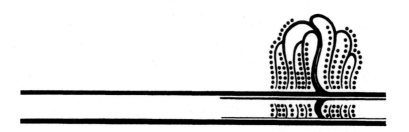

SELECTED BIBLIOGRAPHY
A List of the Works of Yusuf Idris

Novels:

Qissat Hubb ("Love Story"), Cairo, 1956. (First published with the short story collection *Jumhuriyat Farahat.*)
Al-Haram ("The Sinners"), Cairo, 1959.
Al-Aib ("The Improper"), Cairo, 1962.
Rijal wa Thiran ("Men and Bulls"), Cairo, 1964.
Al-Baida ("The Fair One"), Beirut, 1970.

Short Story Collections:

Arkhas Layali ("The Cheapest Nights"), Cairo, 1954.
Jumhuriyat Farahat ("Farahat's Republic"), Cairo, 1956.
A-Laisa Kathalika? ("Isn't That So?"), Cairo, 1957. (Republished under the title *Qa'al-Madina* ["The Slums"], 1970.)
Al-Batal ("The Hero"), Cairo, 1957.
Hadithat Sharaf ("An Incident of Honor"), Beirut, 1958.
Akhir al-Dunya ("The Ends of the Earth"), Cairo, 1961.
Al-Askari al-Aswad ("The Black Policeman"), Cairo, 1962.
Lughat al-Ay Ay ("The Ay Ay Language"), Cairo, 1965.
Al-Naddaha ("The Enchantress"), Cairo, 1969. (Republished with minor variations in Beirut under the title *Mashuq al-Hams* ["Whisper Powder"], 1970.)
Bait min Lahm ("House of Flesh"), Cairo, 1971.

Plays:

Jumhuriyat Farahat ("Farahat's Republic"), Cairo, 1957.
Malik al-Qutn ("The Cotton King"), Cairo, 1957.
Al-Lahza al-Harija ("The Critical Moment"), Cairo, 1958.
Al-Farafir ("The Stooges"), Cairo, 1964.
Al-Mahzala al-Ardiya ("The Terrestrial Comedy"), Cairo, 1969.
Al-Jins al-Thalith ("The Third Race"), Cairo, 1970.

Essay Collections:

Bi-Saraha ghair Mutlaqa ("With Limited Candor"), Cairo, 1968.
Iktishaf Qarra ("Discovery of a Continent"), Cairo, 1972.
Al-Irada ("Will Power"), Cairo, 1977.

Translations into English:

The Cheapest Nights and Other Stories, tr. Wadida Wassef, London, 1978.
In the Eye of the Beholder: Tales of Egyptian Life from the Writings of Yusuf Idris, ed. Roger Allen, Minneapolis, 1978.
Rings of Burnished Brass, tr. Catherine Cobham, London, 1983.